P9-CFP-888
Dear Me,

Dear Me,

Gaylynne Sword

COOK COMMUNICATIONS MINISTRIES
Colorado Springs, Colorado • Paris, Ontario
KINGSWAY COMMUNICATIONS LTD
Eastbourne, England

RiverOak® is an imprint of
Cook Communications Ministries, Colorado Springs, CO 80918
Cook Communications, Paris, Ontario
Kingsway Communications, Eastbourne, England

First Printing, 2005
Printed in the United States of America
1 2 3 4 5 6 7 8 9 10 Printing/Year 09 08 07 06 05

Library of Congress Cataloging-in-Publication Data

Sword, Gaylynne.
Dear me / by Gaylynne Sword.
p. cm.
ISBN 1-58919-024-6 (pbk.)
1. Women--Fiction. 2. Conduct of life--Fiction. 3. Diaries--Authorship--Fiction. I. Title.

PS3619.W67D43 2005
813'.6--dc22

2004030093

Acknowledgments

In memory of my sister, Trina Helene Castleberry.

Thank you to my parents who have always supported me, no matter what. Thanks to Sue Lamp for her encouraging first read and Judy Nelson for early edits. Thank you to Nancy Anderson and Tonya Ruiz for getting me to CBA in Indy and Jeff Dunn for believing in what I've done.

And most of all, thank you to my dear husband, David—perfectly picked by God to complete me. Thank you for always believing in me and patiently waiting while I figured out what I'm supposed to do with my life. I love you. More still.

Prologue

I suppose it's become a habit—a bit of an obsession, these ramblings of mine. A rainbow assortment of journals and notebooks, stacked and shelved in every room of the house.

It's true. I would never be able to find a particular one. But there's only one I've ever wanted to look at or read again: a worn, leather-bound book that sits on the shelf by my bed, next to a dingy soda bottle filled with multi-colored glass stones.

It was the first.

I used to spend a lot of energy trying to forget what is written on its pages. But if I've learned anything, it's that sometimes living can be far too painful to gain the necessary perspective at the time. Now I keep it close at hand—always ready to remind me. The best lessons are found in remembering....

Part One

September 7

I've been sitting here for thirty minutes trying to decide how to do this. I feel like I need to write to someone. Something like a letter. I could start each entry with "Dear Diary." "Dear Diary, today Johnny smiled at me in line at the water fountain, and Becky said that Debbie said that Mike said that he likes me a whole lot...." No, way too juvenile. I am so mature, after all.

Maybe, since I'm trying to get used to praying, I'll start each entry with "Dear God."

But that reminds me of a book I read in the sixth grade by Judy Blume, *Are You There God? It's Me, Margaret*. I don't remember what it was about, but I remember it was the type of book we wrapped up in a brown paper-bag cover to make it look like our English Lit book of the month.

What to do?

I think I'll just write it to myself. After all, that is the point, isn't it? To discover where I went wrong, so I won't do it again. So, there you have it. "Dear Me." A bit egocentric and weird ... perfect for a girl who is spending half her time talking about herself in therapy ... oh, excuse me, *counseling*.

Don't you like that word? Counseling. So much friendlier than *therapy*. Nothing threatening about counseling. Seems like the general consensus, after one swallows several varieties of sleeping pills and antidepressants with a bottle of vodka, is that the individual needs a lot of counseling. I can't argue. Anyway, today at counseling, Doug (if I were in therapy, it would be Dr. Haskill) said, "Since we've worked through a lot of the damage done by the mistakes you've made, I think we're ready to start delving into why you made them in the first place."

"Is that really necessary?"

"Well, Vanessa, it seems logical to assume that if we understand where things started to go wrong, then we've got a better chance of not going there again. Right?"

"Yes. But I'm not going to go there again."

"How do you know?"

"Because I've found Jesus," I said in my best big-haired-TV-evangelist twang.

"Well, yes. But 'we all like sheep have gone astray.' Why don't we try to find out why you strayed so far?"

He's so good.

"Okay. You're the professional. But how do I do it? I've told you before, I don't remember much about growing up. It's all ... I don't know—blotchy."

"That's to be expected. Many people who've been emotionally or physically scarred in the past have trouble remembering details. It's a defense mechanism."

"I don't have any deep, dark, ugly secrets hidden in the depths of my subconscious."

"That's not what I'm suggesting. There are things that happen to all of us that influence our future decisions and relationships. We need to look at these things."

"I buy that."

"Good. I want you to start keeping a journal—"

"Oh, man," I interrupted, with a particularly whiny tone of voice.

"My word. Is it that bad?"

"Yes."

"Explain."

"You have no idea how many times I've tried to keep a journal. I have several perfectly lovely ones, each with only the first few pages covered with the most boring drivel imaginable to man. 'Today I went to work. This lady was really rude ... blah, blah, blah.'"

"This will be different."

"Yeah, right."

"I don't want you to journal about your daily life. Your perspective on now isn't what I'm interested in. I want you to write about growing up, your family, defining moments, things like that. Just start with what first comes to mind and go from there."

"What if I don't want to remember all that stuff?"

"I thought you had nothing to hide?" he said, smiling.

"Touché."

"Don't worry about it, Vanessa. I think you'll like it once you get going. Before you know it, what's happening now will begin to make a lot more sense in light of your past. Like it or not, it's all connected. Like the intricate pieces of a quilt: tiny scrap attached to tiny scrap makes a beautiful piece of art."

"How long have you been waiting to use that analogy?" I asked.

"I've got a journal full of them," he smirked.

"You're so funny."

"Thank you. Now, go get yourself a new journal to add to your collection, and start writing."

"Yes, sir."

"Goodbye, Vanessa. I'll see you next week."

"Yes, sir."

On the way home, I stopped at the Hallmark store and bought this lovely leather-bound notebook and a new pen. I think I have exerted myself enough for one day. I'll continue this assignment tomorrow.

September 8

Dear Me,

"Let's start at the very beginning, a very good place to start. When you read you begin with 'A-B-C,' when you sing you begin with 'do-re-mi' ..." You gotta love *The Sound of Music*. I remember putting on Mom's kitchen apron and twirling down our poppy-covered lawn singing, "The hills are alive with the sound of music, ah-ah-ah-ahh!" Which I guess is as good a place as any to begin, since it seems my propensity toward music was what caused a lot of my problems. If I had been born with a knack for numbers or science—anything Dad considered useful—things might have been different. But I "came out humming a tune," as Mom used to say, and Dad never could accept that. I guess I can't blame him, really. It makes sense when you consider his background.

From what I can piece together from conversations I had with Grandmother Lee and tidbits I overheard here and there, my dad—Grayson Herbert Palmer—was born in a cabin in the redwoods along the Northern California coastline. For generations, his family had been loggers and fishermen. His father worked stripping trees and hauling lumber for the Louisiana-Pacific plywood mill. On the day the rope holding twenty tons of lumber on his truck snapped, Grandmother Lee was left with a tiny life insurance policy, no job, and four growing boys. Knowing they wouldn't survive on a prayer and a song, she quit playing the organ at the Methodist church and began working double shifts at the cookhouse, feeding loggers and bringing home leftovers for her sons. But she still couldn't make ends meet. To help pay the bills, Dad got a job at the lumberyard. Hauling and planking trees replaced his dreams of football and dating. But he worked hard on the job and in school, earning himself a scholarship to Stanford University. I think he wanted to be an architect.

The week before Dad had to leave for college, his brother Patrick—who was supposed to take Dad's place at the lumberyard—took a six-pack to the swimming hole. He was the first to dive in. There hadn't been much rain that year. He was paralyzed from the neck down.

So Dad enrolled at Humboldt State University and got a job at a bank, helping out until the next brother came of age. By then, it was too late to move away. He stayed at the bank. A regular George Bailey.

He didn't complain—he just did what any good son would do. Going to class and to work, rolling pennies for Mrs. Gerald's grandson's fifth birthday, and sixth, and seventh.... And every night as he scrubbed the dirty metallic smell from his hands and joined his brothers at the table for pot roast or meatloaf, his bitterness toward his mother grew. He saw her inability to support the family as weakness, and her weakness as the reason for his misery. Although he was successful at what he did, he never got over what "could have been."

Next, enter Helen Cramer, professor of English Literature at Humboldt State and my mother. Not the happiest of upbringings either, I'm afraid. Her parents were a policeman and an artist. They had tried for years to have a child, and when Mom finally came along, her mother went sort of nuts—obsessing over Mom's health and safety to the point that she wouldn't let Mom play with other children or even sleep in her room by herself. From what I understand, Jackson Cramer was a patient man, but he wanted to sleep with his wife and participate in his daughter's upbringing—things his wife would not allow. When Mom was twelve, Grandpa Jack moved to Oregon and left his house on the coast outside of Arcata in Mom's name.

When Dad met Mom, he didn't care about the contrast of her gauze skirts and leather sandals against his crisp white shirt and wing tips. She was the head of the English department, owned her own home, and was ready to commit to a man who loved her and would not leave. He was ready to make the best out of the life he had been given. I don't suppose either of them were ready for the hazel-eyed, curly-haired girl who arrived nine months after their wedding in the redwoods.

They named me Vanessa Lee Palmer. After his mother.

September 10

Dear Me,

Okay, no messing around or trying to analyze things. I'm just going to say it. Whatever comes to mind, piecey as it may be. "Piecey"—is that a word? I don't think so, but hey, it's my story, so I can make up words if I want.

When do I first remember feeling like a square peg

crammed in the round hole of my dad's world? I must have been around two and a half, pestering Dad to listen to a song I had made up while he was trying to work in his office.

"Why don't you take these and go play school or something?" He handed me a ruler and pencil.

I proceeded to get some pots and pans from the kitchen, lined them up in a row outside his office door, and began banging on them with my pencil and ruler. "How do you like my song, Daddy?" I yelled above the noise.

"Stop making all that racket before I find a better use for that ruler!" he hollered, totally unimpressed by my creativity.

I really wanted to please him. I wanted my daddy to be happy with me. But despite my best efforts, I couldn't help myself. Music was kind of like breathing. So I kept on playing and singing, only I tried to do it when he wasn't around.

What about Mom?

She worked a lot. Evening workshops and tutoring her students after hours took up lots of time. She did drive me to my piano lessons and paid me a compliment when I performed well. But whenever Dad complained about my noise or frivolity, she never stood up for me. "Now keep it down, Vanessa. Daddy is working ... he needs it quiet ... Daddy is on the phone...." Her mother had ignored her father's wishes for so long that he finally left. She didn't want to be alone—she hated being alone. Even watching TV or going to the grocery store, she always wanted someone with her. So she did the good, wifely thing. She supported her husband for better or for worse.

I really don't remember much about life before Jake was born. Jacob Andrew Palmer, with Dad's blue eyes and Mom's thick chestnut hair, was born when I was two and a half. He was smart, he was funny, he was charismatic, he was charmed. Everyone loved Jake. He became everything for each of us, fulfilling each of our needs with his perfection.

Mom used him as an insurance policy against Dad ever leaving her. She had given Dad the perfect gift: a son. I used him as my closest friend, playmate, and biased sounding board for my musical endeavors. Dad used him as an opportunity to vicariously experience all that he had missed when he was a boy. He saw Jake as his one chance to make up for his bad fortune. He saw me as a reminder of everything that was wrong with his life.

Melodramatic aren't I?

Anyway, the more outgoing and athletic Jake became, the more introverted and artistic I grew. I graduated from pots and pans to the piano and eventually discovered the cello after watching Yo-Yo Ma on some PBS special. Jake excelled in everything that involved a ball. When I was in the eighth grade, I stayed in my room and practiced until my fingers were raw and I had earned a seat in the junior symphony orchestra. He did it all. I did one thing and had no interest in doing anything else.

I was single-minded, yet conflicted. I wanted to please my parents, but I wanted nothing to do with the things that seemed to please them. What's a girl to do with such contradictory realities? My solution? Make up a new reality.

That's how I viewed it. I didn't lie. Nothing as dramatic as that. I simply exaggerated a bit, fabricated every now and again. I thought, incorrectly of course, that it would make me a little more palatable to the prudent tastes of my superiors.

Example: When it was time to run laps during PE, I often had a cramp in my leg. Sometimes it became difficult to breathe. If we were picking teams for softball, I'll be darned if that wasn't always the time I just had to go to the bathroom really, really bad. That is why I was always picked after Billy Peleti, the kid with mild cerebral palsy who required crutches for walking, because my classmates knew I wouldn't even try to play well. When Jake asked me to play catch with him and Dad, I had a sprained finger, a headache, stomachache.... Practicing my cello was really the only thing that made my ailments bearable. No wonder I had no friends.

In my defense, I did sacrifice some of my precious time and energy in an attempt to participate in something related to Jake's athletic prowess. My junior year, when he was a freshman on the varsity football team, I joined the Fighting Tiger Marching Band. I endured the itchy, beyond-ugly uniforms and, because of the notable lack of cellos in a marching band, played the cymbals, all in an effort to show support for my jock brother. (And to hang out with the really cute drum major. What was his name? Bruce or Brad or something.) The fact that I turned my cymbals inside out when I hit them square on instead of at an angle during the finale of our homecoming routine, thereby ruining my chances with Bruce/Brad, is not the reason I had to drop out halfway through the season. I was really swamped with all my honors classes. Ha!

I became so good at "altering my reality" that I didn't even know when I did it. Which makes it really convenient, because a lie isn't a lie if you don't know you're lying, right? Truthfully, I don't know why I kept it up, because it didn't really help. Dad still ignored me and Mom still supported Dad. Jake never knew any better but to love me. That was just Jake. He attended all of my performances, he bragged to his friends about how talented I was, and he always tried to get Mom and Dad interested in what I did.

"Dad, you should come hear Vanessa play with this string quartet. She's amazing," he said over dinner one night. "Why don't we all go to her concert tomorrow night?"

"Hmmm.... Well, Son, don't you have the all-star game?"

"No, that's on Saturday."

"Oh. Well ... I've got a meeting with the corporate branch manager tomorrow. Maybe next time." He shook his head and never once looked up from his bowl of vegetarian chili.

Mom didn't say a word.

And though there never seemed to be a convenient next time, I appreciated Jake's effort.

"I'm sorry, Nessa. I'm coming to your concert," he said to me as he dried the Dutch oven I had just washed.

"Don't worry about it. If you have a date or something, it's no big deal."

"I'll bring my date," he said.

That was my Jake.

September 13

Dear Me,

It isn't realistic, but I wonder if things would have turned out differently if I hadn't insisted on going to camp. I know it's futile, even stupid to wonder about it now. But I can't seem to help asking, "What if ...?" What if I had taken up cheerleading instead of the cello? What if I'd been born a boy? What if I had stayed home that summer?

Does every choice we make have the power to change the course of history depending on its wisdom and rightness? Or are we predestined to experience every heartache and hangnail before we ever leave the warm comfort of our mother's womb? Does it really matter what we do after we come out kicking and screaming into the cold, too-bright world? These are the types of questions that keep me up at night. I know it's pointless, but I can't help it. Would my life have been different if I hadn't gone?

But I did go. It was my one small victory.

"No, Vanessa. I don't understand why we are having this conversation again. I said no," repeated my father, three weeks before I graduated from Arcata High.

I had secretly applied to the University of the Pacific in Stockton. It had one of the best conservatories in the state. I was trying, again, to convince him to let me go. "But I can help pay for it. There are lots of jobs in the conservatory. And they have scholarships. I missed the deadline this year, but next year—"

"I said no. You can't get a good education if you are worrying about working hours and paychecks. You can go to Humboldt. Why can't you keep playing in their orchestra?"

"I don't want to just play in a college orchestra, Dad. I want to be a professional. I can't do that here. I need to go to a conservatory."

"Well, that's your problem, Vanessa. You've got to get it out of your head that you can actually make a decent living playing that oversized fiddle of yours. It's not going to happen. You can become a teacher or something useful by going to school here."

"You said Jake can go anywhere he wants."

"Exactly, because he happens to excel at something useful. You aren't going, and I don't want to talk about it again."

He picked up his paper.

I sighed.

"Can I at least go to camp this summer? I have enough to pay for it."

"Whatever. If that will appease you, go ahead. But I don't want to hear anything else about UOP. Agreed?"

"Fine."

So I went. Hooray for me. A lot of good it did.

September 13 Again

Dear Me,

I'm not going to do this journal stuff if I keep waking up like this. I've been up for an hour, thinking about my summer at Camp Cazadero. Trying to remember the details. I guess I should have kept a journal back then. I've heard that if you want to remember your dreams, you should keep a notebook by your bed so you can jot down whatever you remember as soon as you wake up. If not, you know how it is: You try to pull out the images of that really great or strangely wonderful dream, and they're stuck somewhere on the tip of your brain. The harder you try to remember them, the more they fade away, leaving you wondering if you really had the dream at all. That's what camp seems like. It was a wonderful dream that got stuck somewhere between the real and make-believe portions of my brain.

I do remember how exciting it was at the beginning. It was like I had died and gone to band-nerd heaven! For the first time, I was submersed in a sea of like-minded teenagers. We all had a passion for making breath and wood and string and metal and black marks on a page into something magical. We understood that what we accomplished on our own was nothing compared to the beauty of what we could create together. And because of this, friendships were forged quickly.

I am embarrassed to admit that I met my first real boyfriend that summer. There I was—eighteen years old and I had never even kissed a boy. His name was Derek. A red-haired violinist from San Jose. (Or was it San Rafael? Well, it was something like that.)

He was so sweet.

I have vague recollections of leisurely walks on the beach; our first kiss in front of a bonfire, with melted marshmallow stuck to my chin; covert glances during long, tedious rehearsals; the cheap, white teddy bear he presented to me when I was chosen as soloist for our final concert.

"Vanessa Palmer, you have a phone call at the front desk. Vanessa Palmer, you have a call," screeched the loudspeaker one morning over banging breakfast trays and the noisy hum of conversation in the dining hall.

"Go ahead," said Derek. "I'll clear your place and meet you at the practice rooms."

I remember thinking that he was such a gentleman. I tried to imagine Dad clearing Mom's breakfast dishes from the table. Ha! Derek's mom had raised him right.

"Thanks."

I walked quickly to the registration office with that pulsing panicked feeling behind my eyes and forehead. I could not think of a single reason that someone would call.

"Hello." I was telling myself to be calm, but my voice wouldn't cooperate.

"Nessa? Are you all right?"

"Yes. I'm fine. What's wrong?"

"Nothing. I just had to call," said Jake. "We got your invitation. Fancy schmancy, Miss Solo Queen."

"I thought you'd like that," I said, starting to breathe again. I had sent them a gold embossed card, the kind with tissue paper covering the words that read, *A Night of Enchantment Under the Stars. Featuring Vanessa Palmer, cellist. July 4, 8:30 PM.*

"And guess what?"

"What?"

"We're coming."

"You are?"

"Not just me, but Mom and Dad too. I got them to promise."

"But what about the game?"

"It's early this year. The Crabs have to travel to Tennessee or something that night so they want to start the game at nine. I'm pitching you know?"

"Of course you are." Who else would?

"Anyway, I told Dad that if we left after lunch we should have plenty of time to get there. I just thought you'd want to know."

"Thanks a lot. As though I'm not already under enough pressure."

"Don't worry about it, Ness. You'll do great. I miss you."

"Me too. I'll see you then."

"I'll be there, waiting to be stunned by your talent."

"Yeah. We'll see."

"I'd better get going. Can't be late for practice."

"Of course not."

"See ya, Sis."

"See ya."

September 15

Dear Me,

The days leading up to the concert are a blur. As far as the events of that July 4—from what I can recall and have heard over the years since, the day went something like this:

It was unbearably hot. The cooling fog never rolled in off the ocean and the massive redwoods trapped the heat on top of us. We rehearsed outside, praying for breezes that never came, except for those lucky enough to be sitting next to the giant fans positioned at the corners of the stage. We drank warm lemonade out of red plastic cups.

Arcata was even hotter. By the time the townspeople began to gather at the Plaza for the annual Jubilee Celebration, it was already 85 degrees. In a town where the temperature rarely gets out of the low 60s, such an occurrence rightfully gained center stage of all conversation. Banjo playing and the sweet scent of greasy funnel cakes filled the air, along with the crack of bats from the ballpark, where the Humboldt Crabs warmed up for the big game. Every year, our semipro team holds a doubleheader. It's as much a part of our July 4 celebration as fireworks, and this particular year was special: They had asked the high school team to join them for the first game. Jake was scheduled to pitch.

The prospect of eating lukewarm food in a stiflingly hot cafeteria was rather unappetizing, so Derek and I went to Gurneville for lunch. We drove with the top down in Derek's convertible Rabbit, taking the curves in the road toward the ocean like a roller coaster. We stuck our feet in the cold Pacific water. We bought Gatorade at Safeway before heading back to camp.

Jake hit a home run. He hit another. And when it was over, the crowds filed out of the stadium to join the party in the plaza. Dad wanted to stay. He was proud and wanted to slap a few more backs and drink a beer in celebration. But they had to leave by 1:00 PM to make it to the concert. He'd promised Jake. They were picking him up at the high school. He had walked there to change his clothes after the game.

I hated to go back in the practice rooms, but I needed to go over my part a few more times before I got cleaned up for the concert.

Mr. Myles McNaughton and his fishing buddy were on their way to Fort Bragg for the annual Salmon Festival. They had downed a few beers early that morning to beat the heat, and the cooler emptied out faster than they had anticipated. It was so hot. They stopped off in Arcata for a refill. They pumped some gas, bought another couple of cases for the road, and turned on M Street. Myles got sick of Hank Williams Jr. and decided to reach for his Charlie Daniels tape on the floorboard. He ran a stop sign and swerved to keep from hitting Doria Peterson and her three-year-old daughter, wearing matching red, white, and blue sun visors, as they walked toward the plaza. He careened across the road until an old tree stopped him. Jake was in front of that tree. He had stopped to tie his shoe.

"Are you ready to go?" Derek snuck up behind me in the practice room. I had left the door open in hopes of catching a renegade breeze.

"I guess I have to be." I put my bow in my lap.

"You'll be great." He nuzzled my neck.

"Yuck! You don't want to do that. I'm gross." I pushed him away.

"Yes, I do and no, you're not," he said in my ear. "But we'd better get going. You need to drink something and at least eat a snack. The last thing we need is for our star performer to pass out from heat exhaustion and hunger."

"Okay. Let's go."

Dad got mad when he hit standstill traffic a couple blocks from the school. It was throwing him off schedule. He strummed his thumbs on the steering wheel.

"If we don't leave by 1:15, we might as well not go at all. The traffic along the coast is going to be horrendous. Everyone is trying to escape this godforsaken heat."

"What do you think is happening?" Mom strained her neck to see over the truck in front of them. She saw the police lights. "Oh, dear. It must be some kind of accident."

"Come on. Let's go! What is going on up there?" Dad put the car in park and got out. Unable to see, he started walking up the road toward the flashing lights.

Bud McDonald, the police chief still wearing his Arcata Tiger baseball cap, saw Dad coming and quickly moved to stop him.

"Grayson. You need to stay back."

"What's the holdup, Bud? I'm going to be late." Not seeing, or ignoring the look in the man's eyes.

"It's bad, Gray. You need to stay back."

"What's bad?" He kept moving, past the front squad car to the Dodge pickup with Seattle plates that was now attached to a huge pine tree that had been undisturbed for at least a half a century. He thought it was good that the idiot hadn't hit another car; he could have hurt someone.

Then he saw it.

I couldn't find my slip. I didn't want to wear one. It was too hot for such nonsense. But my white blouse was too sheer to wear alone, and I had to wear the blouse with my long, full black skirt. Orchestral uniform. I began to worry that I had forgotten to pack it and started to work up the sweat I had just showered off. I finally spotted it beneath my bed.

Under the front of the truck was a baseball cleat.

"Oh, God," Dad said. "Dear God, he hit someone." He started to circle around to the other side. A paramedic met him.

"You need to stay back, sir. Please. Stay back."

He obeyed. He couldn't move. He heard a scream. Mom's. She knew. She knew it before she ever got out of the car. Mothers know these things. Like she knew that the brown curls poking out beneath the crooked orange baseball cap were Jake's curls.

"No ... oh, God, no!"

I stood outside the tent waiting for their eight o'clock arrival. By twenty after, I heard the oboe's wailing tone and the low murmur of strings and woodwinds gearing up for the opening number. The timpani rumbled and I had to go in. I ran backstage, got a drink of water, and grabbed my cello.

"Where have you been?" Derek came up behind me, looking frantic. "Mr. Lamb is freaking out."

"Oh ... I was just looking for my parents. Dad must

have gotten lost again." I laughed so that I wouldn't cry. Took a deep cleansing breath. Went on stage.

Mom shoved Dad and the paramedic aside to get to her son. She removed his cap and pushed the curls off his forehead. Like she always did when he was sleeping. He *looked* like he was sleeping. Was he just sleeping? She lay down next to him, ignoring the puddle of blood that was seeping into her blouse. She touched his face, listened for his breath. There was none—only silence.

I stepped out onto the stage to the sound of enthusiastic cheering and applause. I thought for a moment that I heard Jake above all the rest. And then the crowd fell silent. All I could hear was my heart thudding in my chest. I scanned the audience, but saw nothing but hazy outlines of humanity and a white blur of fanning programs. Mr. Lamb raised his baton.

Mom raised her head and screamed, "Can't someone *do* something? Why aren't you doing something for him? Somebody help him!" She clutched his hat and fell to the ground. No one came near her. They all knew there was nothing they could do.

I played well. Better than I had expected. I couldn't wait to see my parents. If ever they were going to be impressed, this would be it. When the concert was over, I waited patiently outside the tent for them to come out. Derek's parents brought me a beautiful bouquet of yellow roses. I went back inside, fighting against the current. Maybe they were waiting for me by the stage. They weren't. I turned and started back down the aisle.

Reality started to sink in. They hadn't come.

Dad never moved. He watched his wife as though she was on the evening news—detached from what he saw, numb to what he heard.

"It looks like a DUI, chief," said a cop after pulling one of a dozen or so Michelob bottles off the floorboard of Mr. McNaughton's pickup.

"Read him his rights and cuff him," said Bud.

"He's bleeding, boss."

"I don't care. If he's alive, arrest him."

"What about his buddy? He looks unconscious."

"Put him in the ambulance and then we'll book him. Run a check on them both. What do you want to bet this isn't the first time?"

If this had been the first time, it would have been different. I might have even been worried that they weren't there. But it wasn't. They always found some excuse to miss my performances. Why had I believed it would be any different this time?

"I'm sure there's a good reason they're not here," said Derek. We'd been standing outside the concert hall for thirty minutes.

"They must have gotten lost or something," said his mom, trying to be helpful. "Or maybe traffic was backed up for some reason. You should call the Highway Patrol,

Frank, and see if there are any problems," she said to her husband.

"Oh, don't do that. I'm sure they are just late. Dad's notorious for it."

"Did you check the message board?" asked Derek.

"No, but I'm sure they didn't call. It's okay. They'll be here any minute; there was so much going on at home today." I was proud of how calm I was appearing. My performance was lasting longer than I'd expected.

"Do you want to wait, or should we go on without them?" she asked.

"You all go ahead. They'll probably want to get to their hotel right away, anyway. Maybe we can meet for breakfast in the morning."

"We hate to leave you, dear."

"No, really. It's fine. I'm so tired anyway. You go on."

"Okay, if you're sure."

"I am. Thanks for the roses and everything. It was nice meeting you."

"You come visit us, now. Anytime." She hugged me. Frank nodded and smiled as they got in the car.

Derek held me tight and kissed my forehead. "You were tremendous tonight. You know that, don't you?"

"I guess," I said. "Yeah, I was good, wasn't I?"

"The best. Nothing can take that away from you. Okay?"

"Thank you. I'm going to miss you." I started to cry and was afraid I'd lose control if I didn't get to my room quickly.

"Well, let's worry about that tomorrow. For now, you go in and get some rest."

We kissed.

I never saw him again.

"You should just go home. There's nothing else for you to do here," said the officer in charge.

"I don't want to go anywhere!" Mom screamed.

"Come on, Helen. We've got to leave." Dad didn't know what else to do.

"But my baby, my baby ..." she sobbed with huge convulsions of uncontrollable grief, until she spotted them leading Mr. McNaughton to the squad car. She broke loose from Dad's grip and ran toward him, out of control, screaming, "You murderer! Murderer! You killed my baby! You killed my—"

The officers let her get close enough to strike him twice with the fist that held her baby's baseball cap. Then they put him into the car, pushing down his head. She collapsed like a marionette whose master had dropped its strings. Her hair that was always so neatly fastened in a barrette on the top of her head had come loose, veiling her reddened face.

I fell onto my thin mattress and let go. Like releasing a kink in a garden hose, I allowed myself to cry until I thought all the tears were gone. My face was tight and my eyes felt like sandbags, but somehow I fell asleep.

Dad gently picked Mom up off the ground and wrapped his arms around her. They walked toward the gurney that was being wheeled into the ambulance and stopped several feet back, as though an invisible wall was standing in their way. The paramedics heaved Jake into the back, shut the door, and drove off.

It wasn't until later that evening that Great Aunt Marie reminded everyone that someone needed to get me from camp. No one thought it was wise for my parents to go. She offered, but she was seventy-five and no one wanted her navigating the roads at night. It was decided to wait until morning to decide what to do. I guess no one wanted to call me. What would they say?

Dr. Schafer, the doctor who delivered both Jake and me, left Valium that no one took—except maybe Aunt Marie. For when my parents, having grown tired of lying in bed waiting for sleep they knew would not come, left the house in the middle of the night to come and get me, she didn't hear a thing.

Around six o'clock I was startled out of bed by knocking at my door. My head was pounding and my face was sticky from the tears mixed with the stage makeup I hadn't bothered to wash off.

When I opened the door, it took me a moment to register who was standing there. He was shrunken and hunched over. His hair was tousled. He hadn't shaved. I had never seen Dad unshaven. His eyes were red and swollen, probably looking a lot like mine. He looked old. I suddenly couldn't remember any of the hateful speech I had drafted the night before.

"The concert was last night ..." was all I could say.

"I know, I know. Just get your stuff together. Mother's in the car."

My bags were already packed, waiting at the door. He grabbed my suitcase and walked out. I washed my face and brushed my teeth in the small porcelain sink that stood in the corner of the room. My mind raced. Did Grandma Lee die? Was the bank robbed? Maybe Dad had gotten really drunk at the Jubilee and had slept through my concert. Maybe he looked so bad because he was nursing a hangover and Mom was so angry with him she wouldn't even get out of the car.

By the time I had pulled on my sweats and "Camp Caz'—Making the Redwoods Sing" T-shirt, I was convinced that my latter guess was true. The words to my speech started to come back to me. I walked to the car, threw my bag in the backseat, and stepped in—ready for a fight.

Then I looked at Mom.

She was huddled in the backseat, tears streaming down her face, hugging a baseball cap.

"Jake's dead."

So there it is. The life-changing, defining-moment, big event that "only happens to other people." But it happened to us, and we had no idea how to deal with it. How to live without Jake. The family glue.

I need a walk.

September 16

Dear Me,

I don't remember anything that was said at Jake's funeral. I don't remember the people who filled our house before and after it, though I know there were many, bearing casseroles and Bundt cakes, whispering among themselves, "Seems God always takes the good ones ... and in the prime of his life too." I'll never understand why the two most repulsive things to a person in mourning—strange food and senseless conversation—are the two things people are most willing to provide.

I do remember wondering who would watch *Gilligan's Island* reruns with me, eating popcorn out of the big, yellow ceramic bowl. I remember Grandma Lee trying to feed me a putrid mixture of lukewarm cream of mushroom and golden mushroom soup in an I-heart-My-Dad coffee mug, because the casseroles hadn't arrived yet, and God knows I'd feel bad if I didn't eat. I remember waking in the middle of that first night, startled, thinking I'd had a dream. Then I heard the sounds of my father crying alone in his study, and it was the saddest sound I'd ever heard. I remember how strange it was to have to tell myself to breathe, to walk, to eat. Nothing came naturally.

That's it. I sit back and try to replay the events back in my mind of the first weeks after he died. Trying to recall how I felt or what we said to each other. Did we hug? Cry together? Talk? I don't remember. It's like someone erased it. The tape keeps moving from camp, to the concert, the car, the first night home ... and then black, fuzzy static.

Denial. I suppose that was what it was. The first stage of the grieving process, according to self-help books on such subjects. The problem with us was that we never moved on to step number two. I know that my parents were never taught to cope when they lost their fathers. And I am convinced that you have to be taught what to do with grief. Kind of like toilet training. Someone has got to show you what to do with the stuff. If you're never taught how to deal with the unpleasant, yet unavoidable, feelings of pain, you run around with a smelly mess, praying for someone to clean you up.

Mom covered up with a cause. She never talked about Jake, only about Myles McNaughton, the "scum of the earth who should die for what he did." She stayed at the courthouse for his entire trial. She lobbied for stricter DUI laws and started a M.A.D.D. group. She took a leave of absence from the university.

Dad covered up with work. He stayed at the office as long as possible. When he returned home, he'd take a plate of food and a bottle of brandy to his study where he slept on the couch till he could leave again.

I covered up by leaving. I couldn't stay. Without Jake, all I had left was my music. But with Jake gone, it wasn't the same. It was a cruel reminder of what had been. But I couldn't stand the awful pain we would not mention.

"Mom. Dad, I need to talk to you." It was before dinner, one month after IT happened.

"What is it?" Dad asked, as he filled his plate, eager to escape.

Mom turned and looked at me, pulling a tissue from her cardigan sleeve.

"I'm going to UOP at the end of the month. I've talked to them, and it's all worked out."

They stared.

"I know you said I couldn't go, but I can't stay here. I'll work or whatever if you don't want to pay. I'm going."

Mom's eyes watered. She never cried anymore, just watered. Little bits of damp, twisted tissue fell to the floor. She looked at Dad. He looked out the window toward the ocean before tucking his bottle under his arm and heading out the kitchen door.

"Fine. Go. We'll work out the money later." And he was gone.

Mom poured dressing on her salad and sat down at the table.

I left to take a walk.

September 17

Dear Me,

I used to love Heath candy bars. Mom was somewhat of a health-food nut, so I rarely got to enjoy the twin bars of crunchy toffee covered with chocolate. But I always asked for one when we were at Roland's Market, holding out for the seldom but precious lapses of will in Mom's nutritional conscience.

On one particularly gloomy day I asked, "Mom, can I get a Heath bar?"

"No."

"Please. I haven't had one in *forever*."

"I said no, Vanessa. Now go get me a carton of yogurt. Plain."

On my way to the dairy case, I walked past the candy display, the Heath bars taunting me in my misery. So I took one. I stuffed it in my pants and hurried for the yogurt.

I couldn't wait to get home. Somehow, I thought that it would taste better since it was forbidden. Even illegal! I ran up to my room, closed the door, and ripped into the brown and orange wrapper.

My illicit candy bar hadn't fared well in my flared Ditto jeans. The chocolate was melted and stuck to the inside of the wrapper. The toffee was crumbled. I tried to lick the sides and only managed to get chocolate on my favorite cowl-neck sweater. It was awful. I buried the remains underneath tissues and Ivory soap wrappers in the bathroom wastebasket. My method of acquisition ruined the prize. I never asked for one again.

Same with UOP. I wanted it bad. I'd dreamt about it for over two years. But once I had it, I couldn't enjoy it. I wasn't going because Dad had suddenly come to a deep understanding of my needs. He still thought I was wasting my time, but he just didn't care anymore. All he was hoping was that when I was gone, when he didn't have to see my face every day, he would stop hearing the little voice in his head saying, "It should have been her. Why wasn't it her?"

I went to the University of the Pacific because Jake was dead. Not much victory in that. But I went. I packed the 1977 two-toned Buick LeSabre my parents had bought from Aunt Marie for my graduation present and drove south on Highway 1 and east to Stockton. I went because I hoped that when I was gone I'd stop hearing the little voice in my head that kept saying, *It should have been me. Why wasn't it me?*

Part Two

September 21

Dear Me,

Apparently I have been slacking. I got a lecture from Doug at our session today. He said that what I've done was very healthy and all, but if I didn't keep up with it every day, I'd lose momentum, courage, nerve ... and not get much out of it. He's probably right.

I shall press on. Have courage. Go bravely where no mere mortal has gone before. ...

I drove my Buick to Stockton feeling strangely deflated, yet proud of myself for going forward instead of getting stuck in reverse. With each passing mile, the images that had been my life for eighteen years faded into obscurity, like the view from an airplane as you rise higher and higher. What was once a town, a field, a house, soon becomes a patchwork of green, brown, and blue shapes, covering the ground as far as the eye can see. My house, with its water-worn, gray and green redwood planks that blended perfectly into its backdrop of jagged rocks and ocean, the people there, familiar places and memories, all became circles and squares on the landscape of my memory.

I completely detached myself from home, more so than I think most college students do. I needed a whole new perspective on life to survive without Jake. I decided that I would no longer be controlled by the attitudes of others. I would no longer be bound by the curse of my dreams, my double-X chromosomes, or my name. When I drove through the gates of the University of the Pacific, I entered a world where I would map my own destiny, create my own feelings, conquer my fears. (Talk about melodramatic.) I emerged from my Buick stiff and sweaty and stared up at Grace Hall. The stately old woman of a building, with wrinkled glass eyes and a gaping, toothless mouth, swallowed students whole as they struggled through the doorway with boxes and suitcases. My new home.

I have to admit that despite all of my feigned independence, I had no idea what to expect from college life.

"Why are you here?" Mr. Montgomery, my cello instructor, asked.

I thought it was a trick question.

"Come on now. Why are you here?"

"Because I want to be a musician," I answered hesitantly.

"You're already a musician. You can play this thing, can't you?"

"Yes." I could feel my face getting hot.

"I mean why are you here, at this school, in this conservatory?"

"Because I want to get better."

"Okay. Why?"

To show my dad I'm not a fool, I thought. "To be a professional, I guess," I said.

"Don't guess. 'To be a professional.' What does that mean?"

"To get a job in an orchestra, I guess."

"Don't guess. Know. To make a living doing what you love best. To make a series of black marks on the page tell a story. To make music. That is why you're here."

I shook my head. I was exhausted.

"It can happen, you know. Do you believe that?"

"I gue—"

"Uh-uh." He held up his hand to stop me. "Don't guess. Know. It can happen, if you're willing to work hard and sacrifice a lot. It will happen."

I took a deep breath, confused by the sudden hot pressure of tears behind my eyes.

"Are you ready?"

"Oh, yes."

"Good. Then let's go."

As had always been the case, the music part came easy. I drank up the instruction, eagerly devouring all my professors had to offer. I auditioned and was awarded first chair in the orchestra. (Kudos and a pat on the back for me.) I got a job in the music library, organizing and handing out recordings and sheet music to the students. But I was incredibly lonely, longing for a friend, someone to talk to.

I had assumed it would be easy to find my niche. After all, I was no longer bound by the chains of high school conformity. But there were too many choices. I found them overwhelming. I summarized my theory on this in my first freshman English composition assignment: "To Me College Is ... A Cafeteria."

This bit of profundity came to me while I was standing in the middle of the dining hall trying to decide if I was going to have pizza, a burrito, fried chicken with mashed potatoes, or the salad bar. Growing up, the extent of my culinary choices was Raisin Bran or Cheerios for breakfast. I spent half my lunch break trying to decide which line to stand in.

By the end, I wound up with a slightly soggy turkey sub that I had to inhale, an A- quality essay topic, and the motivation just to take the plunge and choose a line next time.

The social hub in the freshman dorm was the bathroom. Each hall had its own where the girls migrated every morning and night, carrying their baskets filled with shampoo, conditioner, soap, razor, washcloths, and any other feminine necessities. It wasn't uncommon for a group of two or three girls to be camped out on a bench outside of a shower stall just gabbing away, undressed and unashamed.

"Where are you from?" asked a voice from somewhere above my showerhead.

I jumped and poured half of my shampoo down the drain. "What? You scared me," I said, wiping water from my eyes so I could see the freckled face peering down at me.

"I'm sorry. I grew up with six sisters. I never learned the meaning of privacy."

"That's okay." I put some of the salvaged shampoo on my head and tried to turn from her view. "I'm just not used to this yet."

"I'm Lexi. Where are you from?"

"Arcata. It's about nine hours—"

"I know where it is. I'm from Willits. We drive through Arcata on our way to Grandma Pat's in Eugene every year. Cool!"

"Oh, yeah?"

"Everyone I've met so far is from L.A. or San Bernardino or something. I thought I was going to have to bleach my hair blonde and start saying things like, 'It's like ya know' every other sentence just to fit in."

I started rinsing my hair and laughed.

"What'd you say your name was?"

"I didn't. It's Vanessa." I turned off the water, deciding I wouldn't shave my legs in front of my audience, and grabbed my towel. "What's your major?"

"Undeclared. I figured I'd finish my General Ed before making any major commitments. It's driving my mom crazy, but I don't want to keep changing it all the time. What about you?"

"Music performance. I play the cello."

"Uh oh."

"What's that supposed to mean?" I grabbed my robe off the mildew-covered tile and put on my flip-flops.

"You music types are so serious."

"Why do you say that?"

"My roommate plays the bassoon or some awful thing. She hasn't said more than two words to me since she got here. Last night she didn't get in till late so I started razzing her, 'Oooh, did you have a hot date with a tuba player, Joy?' Just giving her a hard time, you know. She just shook her head and said, 'I was practicing. I actually know what I want to do with my life.' Man. What a priss. I think she sleeps with that thing."

"I doubt it, way too pokey."

Now she laughed. "Are you rushing?"

"Excuse me?"

"Rushing a house? You know, the Greeks. There are all kinds of Little Sister parties going on this week, and next week the sorority parties start. My mom's a *Delta Delta Delta*, so I don't have much choice there, being a Legacy and all. But they are really cool here. You want to come with me?"

Though she could have been *talking* Greek for all I knew, I said, "Sure, why not."

"Cool. Tonight's *Sigma Phi*. Little Sister rushing isn't any big deal. Wear something little and smile a lot and you're in. I'll meet you downstairs at eight."

"Okay. Thanks. It's Lexi, right?"

"Like, for sure." She flipped her hair and disappeared into the stall. "See ya!"

I walked down the hall wondering if I had anything little to wear.

I changed my clothes three times before meeting Lexi in the lobby of Grace Hall. She wore a miniskirt and a T-shirt that fell slightly off her shoulder. Her red hair was in a giant ponytail on top of her head and she wore lots of green eye shadow that would have looked ridiculous on anyone else.

"Hey there, girl. Are you ready?" she asked when she saw me.

I wanted to say no. I was wearing a floral sundress that was short but simple and young looking.

"You look great. What I'd do for a figure like yours," she said as we left the dorm.

She was just being nice. "So, you've been to one of these before?"

"Oh yeah, two last week. It's a great way to meet guys and stuff. You'll like it."

"I'm not too good with guys."

"Well, they're not too good with girls, so you don't have anything to worry about," she said, nudging me in the side. "Don't look so nervous. You need a beer."

I needed something.

I could live a thousand years and never understand the appeal of fraternity houses. Fifty bull-headed boys, living like pigs ... there should be some sort of law against it.

"Where you from?" the first pig—I mean boy—I met asked.

"What?" I turned my head away from his beer-pizza-cigarette breath.

"WHERE ARE YOU FROM?" Cupping his hands around his mouth directed the stench, not the sound, more precisely toward my face.

"A small town, six hours north of San Francisco. What about you?"

"San Bernardino, east of L.A. You a freshman?"

"Yeah. What's your name?"

"Peter. The guys call me PJ," he said, turning around to show me his initials on the back of his fraternity jersey, as though I couldn't figure out how to spell PJ. "What about yours?"

"Vanessa—"

"Chug, Chug, Chug! Bong, Bong, Bong!" All conversation in the room suddenly stopped midsentence and everyone began chanting. PJ spilled his beer down my front when he raised his hands to cheer on his buddy, who was drinking beer from a hose with a funnel on top in the middle of the room.

"All right!" He joined the crowd, yelling and clapping as if the guy had achieved world peace. "You want another beer?"

"No thanks."

He took off in the direction of the Holy Keg.

I started looking for Lexi. We had been there an hour, and it was obvious after five minutes that I had definitely picked the wrong line. I was ready to leave.

Two more spilled beers and a supposedly accidental hand on my chest later, I found her, backed up against a wall, giggling at whatever was being shouted into her ear, looking as if she'd not be ready to leave until sometime the next morning.

I fought my way to the door and left by myself.

"What happened to you?" my roommate, Eileen, asked when I finally got back to the dorm.

"Rush."

"Oh. Have fun?"

"No. It was awful. It smelled bad, I couldn't breathe, it was so crowded I couldn't walk, and the only music they played was Depeche Mode."

"What did you expect from a house full of guys, living for the first time without their mamas? With all the beer they want and girls coming over to impress them. Manners?"

"I had no idea what to expect. Believe me, I wouldn't have gone if I did." I stuffed my sundress in my laundry bag, put on my robe, and headed for the showers.

"Wait up. I'll go with you."

Eileen Jameson was an engineering major from Redding. She took her studies seriously, spending most of her time away from the room. We hadn't had much of a chance to get to know each other before that night, but I had assumed we were too different to become friends. She seemed too smart for me and, frankly, a little nerdy. (I was so cool after all....) Anyway, we ended up talking well into the night.

Line number two lasted a little longer than the first.

"Where you going now?" Eileen asked as we left the

cafeteria with our cups of Captain Crunch cereal. I guess we'd been hanging out for a week or so.

"The library. I have a theory test on Thursday."

"Why go tonight? It's only Tuesday."

"I'm not like you. You may glance over your thermonucleo dynamics notes an hour before an exam and ace it, but I have to study the intricate scale structures of 'Mary had a little lamb' for at least two days to have any chance of doing well."

"Yeah, right. I just thought you might like to go with me to my meeting."

"What meeting?"

"It's more like a Bible study, really. We meet in the Student Union at seven."

"Bible study? You mean, like church?"

"No, it's much more low-key than that. We sit around, eat snacks, sing a little. Then we talk about the Bible and what it means in our lives. Why don't you come see for yourself?"

"Thanks, but I can't tonight," I said.

"Okay. Maybe next week."

"Yeah."

She walked toward the Union and I headed toward the library, wondering why her invitation made me feel so uncomfortable.

September 22

Dear Me,

The whole thing really bugged me. I liked Eileen so much. I hated to think that her peacefulness and confidence that I found so appealing came from her religion. Especially if her religion had to do with the Bible. The Bible was for Christians, and I had had a few experiences with Christians—none of them pleasant.

Most notably were the "Three Beautiful Blondes": 2nd runner-up, 1st runner-up, and the Prom Queen herself of Arcata High Class of '85. They hung up posters for God-Squad meetings around campus, while wearing T-shirts that said, "Smile, God loves you." They were honored in the yearbook—pictures of them painting houses on a mission trip to Mexico, with their perfect blonde ponytails sticking out of cute red bandannas. And when they weren't proselytizing Bible study and good works, they could be found in the bathrooms smoking something a bit more sweetly fragrant than Lucky Strikes, cussing up a blue storm.

Then there were the owners of a little Mom-and-Pop store Jake and I frequented after school for forbidden Heath bars and Bubble Yum Bubble Gum. Frieda and Frank something-or-other. They saw every change in the weather or flu epidemic as a sign from God Almighty that He was tired of the sinful nature of our heathen town. They displayed half a black walnut shell on their counter, placed high upon a cigar-box altar, with an index card taped above it bearing the sacred inscription, "Holy Nut: found on the doorstep to our store on the morning we opened. Notice the profile of our Lord Jesus in the center of the nut ... A sign of His blessing on this establishment and those who patronize it. God Bless You All."

Frank and Frieda didn't appreciate it much when I picked up one of the dozen walnut shells outside of their store, right underneath the big tree that had been there for years, and asked them if they saw its remarkable resemblance to Adolf Hitler. They said they'd pray for me.

Hypocrites or harebrains—that's how I viewed Christians. The thought of joining a gathering of them on purpose was ridiculous. Nevertheless, when Eileen asked me if I'd like to join her the next Tuesday, I didn't have a good excuse. It must have been the sugar from all the Cocoa Puffs I'd eaten for dinner. Whatever the reason, I agreed to go.

"I don't know a thing about the Bible."

"All the more reason to study it, don't you think?" Eileen asked.

"Do I have to pray or recite anything?"

"We do ask our male visitors to be circumcised before they come in. We have a little booth set up in the back, but you don't have to worry about that."

"I didn't think engineers had a sense of humor. Especially religious ones," I said.

"Surprise, surprise. I even like to dance!"

"Wonders never cease."

"Come on. If you hate it, you don't have to come back. Heaven forbid, you might even enjoy yourself."

Heaven forbid, I did.

At first.

It was not what I had expected. Admittedly, I felt a little uncomfortable during the singing, since I didn't know the words and they were all about praising Jesus, which seemed rather goofy to me. The get-to-know-you games were silly. But despite my best intentions, I started to enjoy myself. As for the actual Bible study time, we sat in a circle and studied a passage from the Bible. The leader made it easy to understand, no "Thou Arts" or "Hast Begottens." He talked about love and forgiveness and direction in life. I found it all intriguing.

My favorite part came at the end of the meeting. That was when students stood up to share their "testimony" about "coming to know Christ personally." I guess there's something about hearing how people overcome all their personal garbage that makes you feel like there's hope for you after all.

One guy spent much of high school smoking pot and sleeping around, thinking he was indestructible, until he was arrested and realized he had to get his life together. Another's girlfriend committed suicide when she found out she was pregnant. He thought about killing himself until he met Jesus in a shopping mall. One girl thought that the only way to feel good about herself was to sleep with guys, but the guys kept leaving her and her self-esteem got worse and worse. Each of them had reached a point where they thought there wasn't any hope for them, that they'd gone too far, done too much for God to love and forgive them. But each of them found hope and forgiveness and turned their lives around after "accepting Jesus into their hearts." The terminology they used seemed elusive and exclusive of us heathen types, but I couldn't argue with the change that came about from their conversions.

I went for about a month. I probably would have kept going if I hadn't given in to the persistent invitations for dinner from one of the group leaders. I can't remember his name.

"You know, Vanessa, you never know what's going to happen in life. Like a car could hit us right now and you'd be face to face with your eternal destiny." How's that for an opening line of a first date? I was tempted to ask him to turn around, but my Mama raised me to be polite to the menfolk, so I just smiled and nodded my head.

"Do you know what would happen if you died right now? Do you know if you'd go to heaven or hell?"

"I've never really thought about it, I guess," I said.

"Hell's no joke, Vanessa." (*No, hell is this date,* I thought to myself.) "You have to make a decision sooner or later, and you never know when there's gonna be no more chances."

I gave him the Silent Stare (universally interpreted as utter disbelief of what one is hearing).

"Have you ever had anyone close to you die?" he asked.

"Yeah, my brother died a few months ago."

"Well, then you know what I mean—experiences like that make you really start thinking about the hereafter. Last year when my dog died, I realized more than ever how fleeting life is and that I didn't want to miss my opportunity at salvation—" He would have gone on forever.

"Did you say your dog died?"

"Yes. I had had him since I was a boy and ..."

"I told you that my brother died and you compared him to your dog?"

Silent Stare.

"I know it seems different, but the reality is the same, life is short ..."

"And so is this date." (That I really did say.) He gave me the Stare, turned around, and drove me back to my dorm.

I couldn't go back to the Bible study. That guy rekindled my smoldering opinions about Christians into a roaring flame. I started avoiding Eileen as much as possible, making up excuses for not going, eating out on Tuesdays. Being rude and self-righteous.

Eventually, she stopped asking me. I was more than happy to find a new line to stand in.

If I don't go do some laundry right now, I'm going to have to wash out my underwear in the sink tonight. So, I'll continue my saga another time. Tomorrow. For sure.

September 23

Dear Me,

The Greeks were out and the Christians were out, so I gave up trying to fit into a different crowd and returned to my roots, my soul mates—the Music Majors. We musicians are a different breed. A class all our own, so to speak. I suspect that we have our own mansion community set up in heaven, set apart from the accountants and school principals, so as not to disturb anyone during our all-night jam sessions. That's my guess. Anyway, I stopped looking for something different and defaulted to my own kind.

"Why don't you come to the *Phi Mu* meeting tonight? They're picking Sweethearts," Leslie, the second chair cellist, said after rehearsal toward the end of October.

"No thank you, I don't do the Greek thing," I said.

"This isn't really a Greek thing."

"I don't think *Phi* and *Mu* are in the English alphabet."

"Well, it's a professional fraternity."

"I'm sure they all consider themselves professionals."

"It's a music fraternity. All the guys are in the conservatory and they pick Sweethearts from the music department, not as playmates, but contemporaries."

"Yeah, right."

"Come on, Vanessa. Stop being so cynical. I've known a lot of girls who have participated and they really enjoy it. It's not like the others. Do you think I'd be interested in a typical fraternity?"

I looked at the rather plain, tall, and pale girl and agreed it must be different.

"Where do they meet?" I asked.

"Thatcher 217. Eight o'clock."

"What do I wear?"

"Clothes would be good," she said.

"I can do that."

"Hey, there's someone I want you to meet," Leslie said, leading me through the crowd. "Kenneth, this is Vanessa, the cellist I've been telling you about. Vanessa, Kenneth."

"Hello. I've never heard a musician speak so highly of her number one rival; you must be something," he said.

"No. Leslie's just too nice," I said.

"Don't be embarrassed. It's okay to be considered the best if you deserve it," said Kenneth. "I've known Leslie for a while, she's not that nice."

"Thanks a lot," she said. "At that, I'm going to get a Coke."

"You know I'm kidding, Les. Don't go away mad."

"Not mad, just thirsty. You want anything?"

"No," we both said.

"See you guys later then."

"Let's find a quiet spot to talk, Vanessa," he said.

He led me to a vinyl couch in the corner of the room.

I was mortified when my legs made a rude noise as I shifted positions, but Kenneth didn't seem to notice.

He had sandy blond hair and gorgeous green eyes that watched me intently throughout our conversation. Lots of people, mostly girls, stopped by while we talked, but he never showed any desire to allow their interruptions to be permanent. We talked for hours. He was a junior with a double major in piano performance and music management, and I was 100 percent, bonafide-crazy in love.

I left the meeting tired and hoarse from talking for so long. My stomach was dancing a jig and my heart fluttered erratically, somewhere between ecstasy and panic. It was a new feeling. Remember now, my short-lived summer with Derek was the extent of my dating experience thus far. I convinced myself, so I could get some sleep that night, that what I had thought was love was merely girlish infatuation. He was just being nice to a freshman. He'd probably not even remember my name if I ran into him again.

He was waiting outside my classroom when I came out of Music History.

"Hi, Vanessa. And how are you this fine day?" he said.

"Great," I said, trying not to appear as surprised and pleased as I was.

"Had lunch?"

"No. I was on my way to Grace now."

"No you're not. You're coming with me to get something decent to eat. Don't you know what they put in dining-hall food?"

"I try not to think about it," I said.

"I knew you were a smart girl. Have you been to Quido's? Best pizza in town."

"No. Sounds good to me."

"Come on." He took my books.

He carried my books!

"My parents hate that I'm here. They always expected me to go to Julliard," Kenneth said with his mouth full of chicken pesto pizza.

"My parents wanted me to stay home and become a teacher."

"How'd you get out of that one?"

"Well, it's kind of a long story—"

"I thought it would be good to study the business side of performing, along with the art. More marketable you know. I liked the balance of the programs here."

"I never thought of that. I guess it is smart to cover all your bases."

"That's for sure. Mom was the musician and Dad the manager in our family. She ended up with rheumatoid arthritis; barely able to comb her hair, much less play the piano."

"How sad."

"Dad at least finds work wherever he is."

"How's your mom doing now?"

"Better. They moved to Southern California a couple of years ago. The weather seems to help. Dad got her a couple of puppies for her birthday. Some skinny little things, Italian Greyhounds I think they're called.

Wolfgang and Amadeus. Cute, huh? They seem to keep her company. I've been so busy I haven't talked to them in a while."

"I know what you mean. I don't talk to my parents much either. My dad—"

"How long have you played the cello?"

"Uh ... about six years."

"Really? I've been playing since birth. You're good, Vanessa. A natural. I heard you play this morning."

"You did? You sneak into every potential Sweetheart's rehearsals?"

"No, only those who are worth sneaking in on." He had the best smile I'd ever seen. "You put your heart into it, and that's what it takes to make it. We artists have to give up everything in pursuit of our craft. It has to consume us or we might as well quit trying."

"Well, it's all I have."

"How's that pizza?" he asked mid-chew.

I looked down at my plate. I hadn't had a chance to try it.

And so were the days of our lives ...

He took over, assuredly steering us at top speeds toward his goals. There was no time to breathe. He was so sure of himself and so sure of my abilities, I had no reason to doubt anything he said or did. He took over my thoughts, my emotions, my music. He accompanied me at my performances, he picked my music, he scheduled my practice and study time. He encouraged me and boosted my ego whenever needed. He took me out to dinner and bought me clothes with a "more professional quality" to them. He woke me up at 5:30 every morning to go jogging, despite my desperate protests. After all, "if you don't take care of the body, all else is for naught." If I didn't like an outfit he chose or wanted to see a movie instead of practice on a Saturday night, I never said so. It would have been silly to seem ungrateful, right? He knew what was best for me.

"I love you, Vanessa Lee Palmer," he said after we ate Thanksgiving dinner at Marie Callender's. We had decided to stay on campus over the holiday and get some extra practice time while the campus was quiet. "I am so thankful that you've come into my life."

"I love you too, Kenneth. Thank you for letting me into your life."

"It's where you belong."

I believed him.

"And I don't want you so far away anymore." He handed me a small velvet box.

I almost dropped it. "What is it?" I opened it up and stared. At first, I was disappointed and embarrassed, until I realized that what the box held was much better than a ring.

"Move in with me, Vanessa."

I took the silver key to his apartment from the box and held it tight. I moved in before Christmas vacation.

I know it seems stupid, naïve, immoral, and a whole list of other rather unpleasant words ... but I did not consider a one of them. We moved too fast. I was in way over my head. But I believed that I was finally getting my due—love, intimacy, and someone who appreciated my talent. I didn't have to think twice.

September 24

Dear Me,

I didn't see my parents at all during those first four months. Every two weeks, I'd call them to give my obligatory progress report and ask for money, though I didn't need much of it after I hooked up with Kenneth. He took care of everything. I didn't tell them about our cohabitation—I just let them keep on paying the room-and-board expenses that I no longer used. Considerate, wasn't I? Anyway, since we stayed at school for Thanksgiving, I had no excuse not to go home for Christmas. I had mixed feelings about it—I wanted to show off my new world, and I wanted to keep it to myself. It was confusing. As usual, Kenneth came to my rescue.

"You're not going home for Christmas?" I asked.

"No. Mom and Dad are going to be in New York with her sister. I have no desire for that. I'd rather stay here with you." He kissed my neck.

"But you know I'm going home."

"Why?"

"I haven't seen them in four months. I've been avoiding it long enough. I've got to go."

"Why?"

"You're impossible." I slapped him away. "Because I have to. Why don't you come with me?"

"I thought you'd never ask," he said, pulling my hand from the curl I'd formed around my finger, kissing it. "Then I can keep an eye on you while you're gone."

"What are you afraid of?" I asked, flattered.

"That you'll forget to practice the Bach we chose for your recital."

"Oh. What Bach?"

"See what I mean, you've already forgotten. Six Suites?"

"I didn't know you were thinking of it for recital."

"Well, of course. It's perfect. I'll adapt the score for me to accompany you. We'll get started as soon as we get to your house."

"Whatever you say, boss. But you better get busy packing; my boat of a Buick departs in the morning."

"I'm already packed," he said as he led me down the hall.

"I thought you said you had been planning on staying here?"

"I like to be prepared," he said as he pushed me lightly into the soft, plaid-covered duvet that covered his bed.

Always the planner. I never thought to ask the obvious questions then. Why did he already have his bags packed? Why did he always get exactly what he wanted? Why did I let him control every part of my life? I don't know. I guess I just didn't know how to do it on my own. He made me feel safe. He was my savior. A replacement-Jake. Love really is blind. ...

Who knows?

We got to my house in Arcata around three the next day. Everything looked the same, but different. Wrong somehow. I couldn't quite figure out why. We walked in the front door of the eerily quiet house.

"Mom? Dad? We're here."

"Oh, Vanessa. You're earlier than I expected. I'll be right down," Mom yelled from upstairs.

I looked around the front room.

"Hi." She hurried down the stairs. Same mom, smoothing her floral skirt and tugging at her cardigan as she descended. She gave me a hug. Touched my hair. "Look at you, your hair's so long."

"Yeah. Mom, this is Kenneth."

"Of course, Kenneth. I'm so glad you could come."

"Thank you, Mrs. Palmer. I'm happy to be here. I hope the spontaneity of it all didn't put a cramp on your family's Christmas plans. I know you were looking forward to spending some time with Vanessa."

"No, no. We are glad you are here."

"Well, thank you for your hospitality," he said.

"Can I get you anything? You've been driving so long."

"No, Mom. We just ate a little while ago."

"Well, then come sit." She led us into the front room.

It wasn't until we sat on the couch that I realized what was wrong. Back at school, Christmas lights and big plastic Santas had been up since early November. It was the first and only thing I had missed about being away from home. Not getting up early the day after Thanksgiving and hauling the boxes marked "Xmas Stuff" from the attic. Not telling Dad, "a little to your left, no to your right, down a little," as he hung the lights around the porch and awnings.

Christmas hadn't come to the house that year. There were no lights or candles. None of Mom's collection of Santas she'd been growing since we were born. No fresh, slightly bushy Douglas Fir tree, cut down the Saturday after Thanksgiving after hours of searching the tree farm for just the right one. Every year, we all donned blue jeans and rubber boots and went tree hunting. She'd make one of us stand next to a prospect, just in case somebody snatched it up before she had time to decide.

One year, both Jake and I had been perched in front of our respective trees for over a half an hour. Mom told me to go get Jake. Dad was waiting for us by the winner, saw poised and sharpened, ready to cut. I snuck up on Jake. He was facing his tree. He jumped when he heard my boots squish in the mud and zipped up his pants. "I tried to hold it," he said, red-faced. I laughed so hard I almost wet my pants.

Christmas time was the best time of year for the Palmer family.

"Mom, where's the tree? All of your Santas?" I asked.

She looked around. "I've just been so busy this year. I didn't get around to it. With no one around to enjoy them, it's hard to get motivated to drag all that stuff from the attic." She pulled her ever-present tissue from the sleeve of her sweater and wiped her nose. "I didn't know exactly when you were coming and time just got away from me."

"It's okay. It just seems strange."

"I can help you get them down," said Kenneth.

"No," she said more forcefully than I'm sure she intended. "No need for that. It's so close to Christmas anyway. By the time we get them up, it would be time to take them down again."

"Are you sure?"

"Yes, dear. Thank you though."

I was glad he didn't pursue it any further.

"Where's Dad?" I asked.

"The doctor."

"Excuse me?"

"I know, I know. Impossible as it may seem," she said.

"What happened to, 'They're all quacks ... just waiting to get you into their office filled with germs so you get sick and have to come back'?"

"I don't know. He just woke up this morning and told me he was going."

"What's wrong?"

"He's had a bad cough since September, some sort of bronchitis or something. He said it was just the weather, as usual, but now he's so tired of coughing, he finally broke down and went to get some medicine. He should be back soon."

"Has he ever even been to the doctor? Even when Jake broke his arm at football practice, he refused to sit in the waiting room."

Both of us looked stricken at hearing the word "Jake." It just popped out. I didn't realize how strange it was until I heard it, hanging in the air like sulfur, vaguely green and smelly.

"I know," Mom said, trying to recover. "He must be getting old and weak in his convictions. Anyway, why don't you two go get your things out of the car and get settled in while I make some coffee? Kenneth, I made up the hide-a-bed in the spare bedroom. Vanessa will show you where the towels are and all that."

"If it's all the same with you, Ma'am, I'll share a room with Vanessa," he said as casually as if he asked for his coffee with cream.

"Oh. Well, I suppose that's fine. I just ..."

"I'm sure it is awkward to see your little girl all grown up. But I'm so used to having her with me, I don't think I could sleep well at all without her next to me." He wrapped his arms tight around my shoulders. I didn't know where to look but at the ground.

"Okay, then you two get settled and I'll get the coffee." Our eyes met briefly before she turned to the kitchen.

"I can't believe you did that," I said when we got outside to the car.

"What?"

"Said that to my mom. I thought she was going to faint. Did you see how red her face was?"

"I don't care. I'm much too old to be sneaking down the hall, praying the floorboards don't squeak. Having to set an alarm to get back in my bed before the parents get up."

"I'm glad. I just was surprised."

"You shouldn't be surprised. You're mine now. They'll have to get used to it."

"I guess so." I hugged him before grabbing a bag from the trunk.

"I told you everything was going to be fine. Just stick with me."

Dad came home while we were sitting in the kitchen drinking coffee and eating gingerbread cookies that a former student of Mom's had brought by the house. Kenneth was sharing stories about New York, and we didn't hear Dad come in until he started to cough in the entryway. Mom flinched at the sound.

"We're in here, Grayson."

I mustered up my nerve and went to meet him. We hugged awkwardly, like third-cousins once removed (whatever that means) meeting at the semi-annual family reunion. "Hi, Dad. You okay?"

"Fine, fine. And you?"

"Good. Good."

"What did the doctor say, Gray?" asked Mom.

"Oh, nothing I didn't already know. I've got some sort of flu. He gave me a shot of some sort, and I feel lousy." He nodded at Kenneth for the first time.

"I hate medicine myself. I'm Kenneth, sir, glad to meet you." He offered his hand to my father and shook it. "You have a lovely home here. I've never been this far north."

"Well, the sun never shines and the seagulls never shut up, but I guess it is as good a place as any. Where are you from?" He sat down and nibbled on the foot of a gingerbread boy.

"East Coast, actually. But my parents are settled in Southern California now, Orange County. It's sunny, but not nearly as beautiful as this," he said, dramatically waving his arm toward the ocean view.

Dad looked out the bay window. "It's home."

"Well, thank you for welcoming me into your home. I hope to spend more time here in the future."

And with those words, Kenneth paved the way for the most pleasant time I'd ever had with my parents. He had a way about him. I can hardly explain it. It was a type of magnetism—a charisma—that drew people in. I was, obviously, firmly attached. But my parents were sucked in too. Even Dad. Kenneth charmed the pants off of them, to put it simply, and I could not have been more proud. I'd caught myself a keeper!

Dad did not retreat to his office once while we were there. He stayed downstairs with us, asking questions about Kenneth's management major, finally realizing there were some more practical aspects of the music profession. He listened to us play together, a minor miracle that ranked right up there behind the Virgin Birth. "Very nice, you two. Very nice," he said on Christmas Eve. He even patted my shoulder. It was a dream.

Mom was fluttery the whole time he was there. Asking him how he liked his toast, dark or light? *There is a human choice to this?* I marveled. I'd always thought it was up to the toaster. Two percent or whole milk? Butter or cheese sauce with your broccoli? She doted all over him. It was great.

"I don't know what you were so worried about with your parents. They're fantastic."

"You're fantastic."

"Well ... what can I say?"

Nothing, not a word.

I hated to leave that New Year's Eve. But we had to get back to work. I didn't want the magic to end—the magic Kenneth conjured with his mere presence. I knew we'd never have another time like that Christmas. I don't know why. I just did.

September 25

Dear Me,

I don't really want to talk about this anymore. I've been sitting here staring at the blank page for an hour. I'm embarrassed at how clearly pathetic I was. Thinking I had gained all kinds of confidence and control over my life, when in reality I was strapped at the hip to an ultra-talented, conceited, control freak who did little, if anything, without ulterior motives. But I know there is no more hiding from the reality of myself. My old self that is!

I did nothing outside of breathing and the occasional bathroom break without asking his permission. I made no other friends, went nowhere, and thought about nothing besides Kenneth Broderick. And it didn't even bother me. Well, that's not entirely true. *Once* it really bothered me, but I never said anything. Heaven forbid I ever express an opinion on something.

I had planned a big surprise for him. It must have been for something lame like our six-month anniversary. I bought tickets for *Les Mis* and made reservations at this little hotel on Union Square. I made up some story about needing to go to the San Fran Conservatory to pick out some music. When I revealed my big surprise, he was actually disappointed that we weren't going music shopping. He'd seen *Les Mis* so many times before he didn't want to go again. Never mind that I hadn't seen it. He sold our tickets and took me shopping anyway. Of course, he then took me to the Sir Francis Drake, which made my hotel choice look like a Motel 6, hand-fed me chocolate-covered strawberries, and ran my hot bubble bath. He did like my choice of lingerie, as I recall. But I think it best I don't travel down that segment of Memory Lane!

Anyway, as always, Kenneth managed to do something charming and sweet to overcome any frustration I might have over having absolutely no say in anything that happened in our lives. Everything always turned out just right when he was in charge. I never had a reason to doubt him. Never.

I want to use that as an excuse for the rest of the story. I tried for years to use it. He had always been right before, he had always known what was best for me, why would I have reason to question him on anything? But that really doesn't fly. It never did.

So, here goes. The meat and potatoes of this whole Kenneth saga ... I never went to the doctor to get on the pill like Kenneth had told me to. I had a tremendous fear of such doctors poking where no one should be prodding. I suppose Mom's mom had never enlightened her about this whole aspect of our gender, so she had never said two words of assurance to me. Remarkably, this small oversight didn't catch up with me until the middle of April, when my very regular monthly friend missed her cue.

I ignored it for a while. Finals were coming up, we were busy preparing for my jury performances. It just wasn't a good time. I planned to tell him the night before we were scheduled to leave for our respective homes at the end of the semester. I was going to take some of my stuff back to Arcata, he was going to see his parents for the first time all year, and then we were going to meet back at UOP to be camp counselors at the summer music camp.

I fixed a fancy dinner, shrimp scampi, and got myself a new dress. Then I waited like a soap-opera diva while the food got cold and I watched the clock meander around at a snail's pace. I was good and mad by the time he got home, three hours later than expected.

"What are you smiling about?" I asked, trying to stay angry in spite of that smile of his. "I've been waiting for hours. I fixed scampi."

"I'm sorry, Van. Don't be mad. I have a surprise for

you. Come here." He took my hand and led me to the living room. "Ta da!"

Leaning against the green plaid couch was a brand-new cello and bow. I stood there stunned.

"What is it?" I asked.

"It's a cello. What do you think it is?" he asked.

"I know it's a cello, but what is it doing in our living room?"

"It's for you. You are the best and you deserve the best. You can't build a first-class career with a second-class instrument. I know it's not a Stradivarius, but ... what do you think?" He pushed me toward it.

I picked up the bow and ran my fingers down the honey-colored face of the most beautiful instrument I had ever seen. I cried.

There was no way I could tell him of my surprise, not when he was so excited about his. Instead, we ate cold scampi and I played him a little Mozart.

September 27

Dear Me,

Okay, so I'm home for two weeks, it's the beginning of June, and I still haven't told Kenneth that I'm pregnant. Not the best of situations. But I wasn't worried.

His influence on my parents remained. They were friendly and interested in me, asking me what our plans were, when they could come down and hear us play. I made up a whole image in my head, like the little plastic people in a doll house: Dad, Mom, Baby, and dog in a perfect house with a perfect car that never breaks down and a tree that never loses its leaves in the front yard. I'd take a semester off, teach cello lessons, Kenneth would graduate, I'd take classes at night. We'd travel together, touring and performing to packed houses in San Francisco, New York, L.A. What a cultured little baby we would have. We'd be perfect. I was actually excited to tell him about it the day we got back to Stockton.

"How did this happen?" he asked.

"Well, there's this little thing called the birds and the bees," I said, trying to remain lighthearted. The look in his eyes was scaring me.

"I'm aware of that, Van. How did you let this happen? I thought you were going to take care of this possibility."

"I guess I lost my nerve about going to the doctor. Then I kind of just got busy and forgot about it. I know it was irresponsible of me. I'm sorry."

"Sorry? Do you realize what you've done here? Everything we've been working for ... does it mean nothing to you?" His voice was getting louder with each word.

I looked around the little restaurant, the place he took me to lunch when we first met. I thought it'd be sweet. All of the confidence I had built up over the two weeks away from him rushed out like air from a balloon released before it'd been tied. I couldn't say anything. I stared into my salad bowl while tears rolled down my deflated countenance.

Kenneth sat, watching me. He closed his eyes and took a deep breath. I could just hear his instructors in the back of his mind: "Take control, you're the master of your music, don't let it control you." He opened his eyes and the anger had left. They were the cool green that captured me from the start. Controlled.

"Don't cry, Van." He handed me a napkin. "It's going to be okay. I'm sorry I got so angry."

I couldn't look up.

"We'll take care of it. I was just so surprised. Please don't cry."

I looked up and he smiled at me. He took my hand and wiped away my tears. "Shh ... it's going to be okay." Visions of night classes and cello lessons returned.

He continued, "There's this clinic right behind the school. I heard some girls in choir talking about it. I'll call in the morning and get you an appointment. We've got a few days until the kids come for camp. I'm sure you'll be feeling fine by then."

I almost told him that I was feeling really good already. No morning sickness or anything. Then it dawned on me.

I stared at him with what I'm sure was a really dumb look on my face while he resumed eating his minestrone. He looked pleased. Relieved. Like someone who had just removed a pesky piece of apple peel from his teeth.

I wondered how I was going to make it out of the restaurant without spewing all over the blue-checkered floor. I squirmed in my chair and unsnapped my jeans. They were getting tight.

Abortion had never entered my mind. Never once. I didn't have any moral objections to it. I was all for choice, women's rights, and all that. I turned the news off in disgust whenever they showed crazy, sign-toting zealots screaming about murder and showing horrendous pictures that no one wants to see. But I never considered it for us. In my mind it was for fifteen-year-olds whose backseat groping went too far, or girls who had been raped. Not for two people in love who had made a child in the right way, just at the wrong time.

I had no idea what to expect. I had no idea how I would go through with it—I was afraid to go get the pill, for goodness sake! I was scared. But I was more scared by the thought of losing Kenneth, and I knew in my heart that I would lose him if I did not go through with it. He never said that. I assumed it. He had his plan for us. It did not include a baby. Therefore, it would not include a baby. End of discussion.

I never even tried to change his mind.

September 28

Dear Me,

I've been debating about how much detail to share about this. It took so long for me even to admit that it happened, much less talk about it honestly. I think it needs to be talked about, but no one ever really wants to discuss it. We like to debate it, defend it, denounce it—but who wants to declare it as a reality in her own life? Not many.

I HAD AN ABORTION. There. I wouldn't put it on a T-shirt, but I don't want to hide behind a bunch of feel-good euphemisms for choice and reproductive rights. The reality is that it took care of one problem but opened the door for many more. There had to have been a better way. But I didn't see any at the time. I didn't even look.

"I've got us an appointment for two o'clock," Kenneth said the next afternoon.

"Today?" I asked.

"Yes, Van. We can't wait any longer or you won't be ready for the campers at the end of the week."

"I know, but—"

"Don't look so worried. I'll be with you the whole time. In a few hours, this will all be behind us."

"Okay." I've never wanted to believe something more in my entire life.

We sat, hand in hand, at the Center for Women's Health and Wellness. I remember in clear detail the others who were there that day. A thirty-something executive in a tailored business suit and red pumps who kept stepping outside for a cigarette. The other was a bewildered girl, no more than fifteen, sitting with her mother. She should have been swimming at the community center or hanging out at the mall, giggling with her friends, not sitting in that gray, dreary place. The mother was flipping through a magazine trying to ignore the huge tears that silently ran down her daughter's face. Nobody looked at each other. We looked at the floor, outdated magazines, the faded walls. Even the tired blond receptionist behind the sliding-glass window had developed the talent of talking to your eyebrows and forehead.

I remember feeling lucky. At least I had my man with me. The "father." He was right there beside me, holding my hand and smiling. He loved me. He would take care of me.

And then the woman called me back for counseling.

We sat on a vinyl couch in a small office decorated with framed posters of teenage girls, looking peaceful and serene, stating, *Your Body, Your Brain, Your Choice.* or, *Be Informed ... Be Educated ... It's Only Natural.* The counselor came in, all smiles and sunshine, taking the edge off the uneasiness that turned my stomach. She asked us how we heard about the clinic and if we were here for birth control or abortion counseling. When I whispered, "The latter," she said, "Wonderful."

She asked about my history, my last period, how

many partners I'd had, and what symptoms I'd been experiencing. She then went on to explain the procedure.

"We'll take you down the hall for a sonogram to determine exactly how far along you are. From what I can figure, you'll probably need to have some Laminaria. It's a type of medication that helps open up the cervix so the instruments of evacuation can be inserted more easily," she said, answering our unasked question. "You'll go home and rest tonight. You'll have a little cramping. Don't worry, that just means the Laminaria is doing it's job. Don't eat after midnight, don't have sex," she grinned, "and be back here tomorrow at eight." She finally took a breath. "Any questions?"

"Two," Kenneth said very professionally. "How much will it cost, and how long until she'll be back on her feet?"

"Well, the pay will be determined by the sonogram. Here is a list of the general fees. As far as recovery, she should be ready to go home a couple hours after the procedure and be back to normal activity in a couple of days. Barring any complications, of course."

"What complications?" I asked.

She put her warm hand on my cold one and said, "Oh, honey, we do hundreds of these a month and only one or two get a little infection or some extra bleeding. It is so rare I hate to mention it. But I have to. Don't worry. It is ten times safer than actual childbirth. And if anything does happen—which it won't—we are all trained here to deal with it. You'll see. When all is said and done, you'll feel so much better."

"But will it hurt?"

"You will be a little uncomfortable. Everyone is different. Some compare it to bad menstrual cramps. We'll give you something for the pain while you are here and when you leave. You'll be just fine."

She sounded so sure. Kenneth was so sure. I smiled faintly and said, "Okay." Sure.

The sonogram determined that I was fifteen weeks along. Kenneth looked at the pricing sheet. I knew it was costing more than he expected. He folded it back up, smiled, and patted my arm, He'd take care of it. No problem.

The doctor inserted three short skewers of seaweed—I can't think of any other way to describe them—into my cervix. "You're all set," he said. "See you in the morning then."

"Everything is going to be fine, Van. I promise."

"I know. Do you think it will hurt?"

"She said it wouldn't be that bad. A lot better than childbirth, that's for sure."

"Well, at least after that you have something to show for your pain and effort."

"After this, the fact that you have nothing to show will be our reward. Thank God. Like she said, when it's all done you'll realize it was for the best. What else could we do?"

"I know ... I know you're right."

"We'll be right back on track before you know it."

"I love you."

"I love you too, Van. It will be over soon."

I went to our room as soon as we got home, put on my nightgown, and went to bed. Kenneth asked if I was going to want to eat a little something. I said no. He went to the practice rooms. I lay in bed and felt the cramps begin to intensify. I was unable to sleep, yet unable to get up. I stayed perfectly still, trying to keep my mind from thinking and my body from feeling what was happening.

Kenneth came in late. I pretended to be asleep. He stroked my hair until he fell into a deep, peaceful sleep. Between the cramping and the nerves, I did not sleep at all. I'm sure Kenneth was puzzled by my red, swollen eyes the next morning after an apparent fourteen hours of sleep.

There were several people in the waiting room the next morning. The whole atmosphere was rushed. They called my name after about fifteen minutes and put me in a room where I put on a gown and took a sedative. The nurse explained that I might hear some loud noises and feel some discomfort, but it would be over quickly and they would take good care of me. Kenneth went back to the lobby. I was ushered into the procedure room and laid down on a cold table with my feet in stirrups.

Things were not as easy as they had said. Apparently, they had not used enough Laminaria and they had to do a lot of manual dilation. The pain was excruciating, as if all of my insides were being torn out. Sometime after they started scraping, I passed out and woke up in another room with Kenneth trying to get me to drink some orange juice. I couldn't believe it when the doctor came in, checked me out, and told me I could go home. If nothing else, they were right about it being over quickly.

Because the dilation hadn't gone as smoothly as they had expected, I bled for four days and had to rely heavily on the pain medication they prescribed. I was thankful for the pills. They helped me to sleep without dreaming.

Kenneth was loving and gentle the entire time, telling the camp organizers that I had the flu and letting me stay in bed for as long as I needed. He kept telling me how proud he was of me. How brave I was. How I'd feel better soon.

He was right, for the most part. By the end of the week, I was feeling well enough to get out of bed. I hated sitting around dwelling on the whole thing, so I kept busy with camp activities and counselor duties. As long as I had something to do, I was okay.

A week after the abortion, I went to the doctor and got a clean bill of health and some birth control pills. As I left the office, I realized that the heaviness in my stomach that had been there for weeks was gone. I was relieved that it was over. It seemed as though Kenneth had been right all along. I had survived. Our "problem" was gone. We could proceed with our plans.

This is the first time I've ever told the whole story from start to finish. Won't Doug be proud? Speaking of Doug, I'd better get going or I'll be late for our appointment.

September 29

Dear Me,

Doug *was* proud. He asked me how I felt. I said I was proud too. Why? Because I told the whole story without falling into a blue funk of reproach. I must be making progress. So, since I just condensed an hour-long session into three sentences, I will continue to condense months of my life into a few short paragraphs.

The feeling of relief lasted throughout that summer. But as classes started up again and the demands of school and performing mounted, the relief was replaced by irrational fear. Anxiety attacks, I guess. The first happened when I was standing in line at registration, skimming through the catalog trying to choose two elective courses. *Modern dance or ballet? Literature of the '20s or Shakespeare?* My heart and my head began pounding, my hands began to sweat. I was having a full-fledged panic attack.

"Next."

What is wrong with me?

"Next please. Honey, you're next."

The person behind me tapped my shoulder and pointed to the old woman whose eyebrows were penciled too high and thin for her wrinkled face. She looked either scared or confused. I knew how she felt. I stared at her for what seemed like an eternity and then mumbled, "Go ahead" to the impatient *Phi Delt* who pushed his way past me with a huff.

I ran outside.

I needed Kenneth. He hadn't told me what classes I should take. *Where is he now?* I tried to remember. I needed him to help me figure it out.

It happened again at lunch. Burritos or deli sandwich? And again when we went for frozen yogurt that night.

"What kind do you want?" Kenneth asked.

"I don't know, whatever. You pick."

I didn't want to tell him about it. He'd think I was crazy. *I* thought I was crazy. The possibility of being alone and making choices terrified me. I wanted to be with Kenneth all the time. I clung to his arm as we walked back to our apartment with our waffle cones filled with peach yogurt. I hate peach yogurt—I'm a chocolate kind of gal.

I started following him around, meeting him outside his classes, waiting outside his practice room. At first, I think he was flattered: "You just can't get enough of me, can you?"

"Nope." I'd kiss him and grab on to his arm.

"But don't you have classes to go to, or rehearsals?"

"I'm going. I just wanted to see you first."

"I'll see you tonight. How about pizza for dinner?"

"Whatever."

"Are you okay?" he'd ask.

"Yeah, fine. See ya."

"Bye."

I'd watch him walk away without looking back and check my watch to see how long until dinner. The days seemed endless.

"Where do you want to go tonight?"

"I don't care. Whatever you want."

"What piece are you going to play for Professor Bundy?"

"I don't know. What do you think?"

"Just pick a dress and come on. We're going to be late."

"Is this one okay?"

"Fine. Now come on."

"I'm sorry."

"It's okay. You just seem so distracted all the time. Like you can't decide which way is what."

"Yeah, I know. I feel that way."

"Well snap out of it, silly. We've got lots of work to do." He kissed the top of my head. "Let's go."

Things just got worse. Every area of my life became affected. My grades started to decline. I no longer trusted my instincts in answering questions on tests. I would agonize over answers for so long that I often did not finish. Taking a firm stand on issues in philosophy was impossible. I couldn't tell you the significance of the contrast between light and dark in Conrad's *Heart of Darkness*. I had to ask Kenneth what he thought. By the time mid-term grades came out, my advisor, a short, bald cellist who had once played with the Boston Philharmonic, called me into his office.

"Miss Palmer, I'm deeply troubled by your marks so far this semester. You have dropped at least one and a half letter grades in every class. What's going on?"

"I don't know, sir. I'm just having trouble focusing I guess."

"You know I'm here to help. Do you want to talk about anything? You look tired."

"No. Everything is fine. I'm just kind of out of it lately. I don't know why."

"You are a bright and talented young lady, Vanessa. You've got a great future ahead of you. Don't let college life interfere with the big picture of why you are here. It's okay to have fun, but you have more to offer than what you've shown so far this semester."

"I know. I'll do better from now on. I promise."

"I'll be checking up on you. Please, come see me if you want to talk. That's why I'm here. And stop staying out so late, or you'll start looking like me. I'm only twenty-nine you know," he said laughing as he slicked back what was left of his gray hair.

"I will. Thank you, sir." It took every ounce of my energy just to smile weakly at his joke.

He had no idea how tired I was.

Not long after my panic attacks started, my ability to sleep ended. With the help of Nytol, I would finally lose consciousness around 1:00 or 2:00 AM. But those first blissful black moments would gradually give way to grays and whites, then reds and blues, and finally the familiar oranges of the poppies growing around my front porch. And the dream would start ...

I was rocking in a high-backed chair, cooing and singing "The Itsy-Bitsy Spider" to a dark-haired baby boy whose little face looked just like Jake's. Out in the field of poppies stood Kenneth, calling my name and beckoning me with his hand, "Come on, Van. We're going to be late. We've got to get going, come on, come on." I looked down at my smiling baby, who kept twisting his chubby fingers in my hair, and back out at Kenneth, who was yelling louder and growing angrier. Finally, I gently put the baby down on the rocker, planning to go tell Kenneth that he'd have to go on without me. But as soon as I stepped off the porch, I heard a bone-chilling scream. I turned to see my baby falling to the floor. I lunged forward to catch him, but it was always too late. He shattered like glass into hundreds of bloody pieces. All the while, Kenneth was yelling, "Come on, Van. Don't worry about him, he'll be fine. We'll come back and get him later. Come on, Van ..."

I would wake up cold and shivering in my sweat and tears. I wanted to grab onto Kenneth for comfort, to somehow steal some of the peacefulness of his sleep. But at the same time, I wanted to run as far away as possible from the repulsive memory of him that was etched in my mind. I couldn't go back to sleep after the dream. I was scared to. I knew that it would come back. It always did.

Kenneth was oblivious to all of it. To him, it was just as he said it would be. Our problem was solved and life was going on as planned. I think he liked my obsessive dependence on him. It was his nature to take control of things, and with me unable or unwilling to make my own choices, it was that much easier for him to do his job. I was very pliable and trusting. I did not tell him about my dream or my falling grades. I knew what he would say: "Oh, Van. Come on. What's done is done, and now you've got to pull it together. We've come so far. If you need help with some classes, just let me know. I'll help you."

I wanted him to help me. But I knew deep inside that no one could.

"I've got some great news for you. I'll be home in an hour." He hung up the phone before I could say a word.

I sat on the couch watching *Oprah* till he came home.

"You won't believe it! I was talking to Professor Mikelson about you missing the San Francisco Symphony Youth Orchestra audition last year and how you were more than ready to start training with some professionals. He said he had a friend of a friend or something who worked in the office there, and he would give him a call. I figured he was just being polite, but today after class he gave me this number and said they were waiting for our call. The principal cellist was in some sort of an accident, and they have a seat they want to fill right away."

"Oh, my gosh." My face was burning.

"You audition Saturday morning! Can you believe it?"

"Saturday? What ..."

"Don't look so scared. This is our big break, Van. If you play with them until graduation, you'll have a sure seat in the symphony."

"What will I play? I'm not ready, Kenneth."

"What do you mean you aren't ready? This is exactly what we've been working toward."

"I know, but not now. I've been so off-kilter lately."

"Exactly why you need to do this. You need a challenge, something to jump-start your confidence. You are ready; you just need to break out and go for it."

"But Saturday? Couldn't they give us a little more time?"

"No, they couldn't. They are touring New York during Christmas break. New York, Van. I told you we'd go together someday. This is it, I'm telling you."

He was so excited, it made me cry. I wanted so badly to share in his enthusiasm. But fear stole all excitement and kept me from seeing that my dream had come true.

"What is it, Vanessa? I've just told you the greatest news ever, but you look like you're about to vomit."

"I'm just surprised and scared, Kenneth. I don't know if I'm ready for this right now. What if I blow it? What should I play? How much do I have to perform?"

"You can play everything from last year's recital. That's the best you've got right now. And they'll ask you to sight-read something. It's a piece of cake, Van. I'll be right there cheering you on. As always."

"Thank you, Kenneth. You do too much for me." I

buried my head in his broad shoulder, trying to feel the warmth that I had always treasured there.

"What are you crying about? This is good news," he said.

"I know. I just feel so unworthy of the chance. What if I blow it?"

"You're not going to blow it. How could you? You're the best."

I spent every hour possible practicing for that audition. I tried to get back the heart that had made my music special. But there was only darkness. Musicians are trained to use emotions, good and bad, as fuel for the music. To visualize pain when the music sounds sorrowful, to find delight when the notes are joyful. My problem was that the pain was so deep, I couldn't control it. If I let my mind wander to where I had hidden my secret, I would get lost and the music would stop completely. I'd find myself crying in the middle of a passage, unable to get a hold of myself. Joy was nowhere to be found.

Kenneth thought it was just nerves. He was confident that I would pull it together when I had to.

Of course I had to. It was what we'd been waiting for. It was why I was there.

The audition was at Davies Symphony Hall. Since this was an impromptu audition, for some reason I had assumed that it would be less formal. I had envisioned going into a room with the conductor and Kenneth and playing casually, as though I were practicing. Instead, I was led onto the stage of the immaculate concert hall where opera legends and virtuosos performed night after night.

I just stood there, stunned, shielding my eyes from the glare of the spotlights hanging from the ornate ceiling.

"You may sit down, Miss Palmer," said a faceless voice coming from somewhere in the middle of a sea of velvet-covered seats.

I looked toward the voice and then to stage right where Kenneth was standing, smiling the encouraging smile that had always given me strength and motioning me toward the chair and music stand behind me.

"Yes, I'm sorry," I mumbled, placing my music on the stand.

"Whenever you're ready, Miss Palmer," said The Voice. "What will you be starting with today?"

Why did it have to do that? Why didn't The Voice just tell me what to do? My mind started racing. Should I start with the easiest piece, to gain confidence and control? Or would that be too boring, leaving a bad first impression? What if I blew a tricky opening number and lost what confidence I did have? Or what if I got too comfortable playing the easy passages and let down my guard for the harder ones? Why didn't Kenneth tell me what to do before I got out here? Why did he leave me stranded like this?

"Miss Palmer? Whenever you're ready. Go ahead."

I just stared.

"Miss Palmer?"

I could not lift my bow. It felt like there were shackles around my wrist. I let it drop. Laid down my cello. And exited stage left.

Behind me I could hear Kenneth scrambling out on stage, picking up my cello and apologizing to The Voice that was now silent. "She must be sick, I'm so sorry, I don't know what's wrong, just give me a minute, I'll get her."

"What do you think you're doing, Vanessa?" he asked.

"Leaving."

"Leaving? May I ask why?"

"Because I cannot play for them. I cannot play for you. I cannot play."

"Yes, you can. Now come on. They won't wait."

"I don't want them to wait. I can't play. I just want to go home."

"Home? Come on, Vanessa. This is it. Get a hold of yourself and come on."

"I can't."

"You can't? Just like that? You're going to throw it all away?"

"It's already gone, Kenneth. I'm sorry."

"Get yourself home then. You know they won't consider listening to you again?"

"It doesn't matter."

"Yes, it does, Van. This was your chance."

I took a bus to Stockton.

September 30

Dear Me,

Remembering that whole scene almost makes me laugh now. It's like a bad movie. Poor Kenneth. He had no idea what was going on.

I did not know what to expect that night. I didn't even know if I would ever see him again. The look on his face was one of such disgust and embarrassment that I figured he would not be able to stand the sight of me for quite some time. It was as if I had performed some lewd and lascivious act in front of his entire family. I was surprised when he came in the door of our apartment around midnight.

"I'm sorry, Ken—"

"Shh. I don't want to talk about it."

"But I need to tell you—"

"No. Please. In the morning." He walked to the bedroom and shut the door.

I was relieved in a way. I had no idea what I needed or could say to him. Everything I said inside my head sounded so stupid. *I was scared to make the wrong decision and really blow my audition.* Like I hadn't blown it anyway?

I slept sporadically on the couch. I had learned how to

wake myself up just before I entered deep sleep to avoid the dream. I'd be asleep for half an hour, then awake an hour, asleep, awake, until I finally decided it was easier just to stay awake.

"You could have come to bed."

"I didn't want to disturb you."

"I didn't sleep much anyway. I just kept going over and over in my mind what could have gotten into you. I just don't get it, Van."

"I know you don't. I don't really either. I just got scared."

"Scared? You've played that stuff perfectly a hundred times before. Never was so much at stake. What were you afraid of?"

"Blowing it, disappointing you, or making it and then realizing that I don't really have what it takes ... lots of things."

"Well you succeeded at most of those things," he said.

"I know. I'm so sorry."

"So am I. I don't know what we're going to do now. I couldn't talk to them after you left. I didn't know what to say," he said to the piece of toast he was buttering.

"Maybe next year when I'm feeling better I can try again. Or maybe Oakland. They have a good orchestra, don't they?"

"But next year you will be almost too old and only eligible for one year of training. This was the year. When are you going to feel better, Van? What is so bad that you threw this away?"

"I don't know. I'm just having trouble getting things together."

I didn't know how to explain it. *Well, you see, Kenneth, if killing our baby was a good decision, I have trouble imagining what a bad decision would be. Therefore, I prefer making no decisions at all.* Sure.

"Well, that's obvious. I'm sure all that you went through was difficult. I don't claim to understand what a woman feels. But it's over, Vanessa. You've got to get on with things before you throw away every chance you'll ever have."

"I know."

"I don't know if we can ever make up for this."

"I know. I'm so sorry."

"Stop saying that. It's over and can't be changed. Let's just move on, okay?"

Sure.

We played the game for about a month. We slept in the same bed, ate at the same table, but our lives were no longer on the same path. We didn't move on. He no longer encouraged me to practice or recommended pieces for me to play. He didn't talk about future plans and stayed away from the apartment more and more. I tried to ignore it. I told myself that he was just busy, distracted by his graduation coming up. But I knew that he was gone. I had driven him away.

One night, I waited in our apartment for him to come home for dinner. When he didn't arrive by eight, I decided to go look for him. Figuring that he had gotten lost in practice for his final jury performance, I walked into the hot practice-room building, remembering the nights we had stayed there lost in our love and our dreams.

As I got closer to his practice room, I heard a beautiful concerto. I had not heard him play it before, so I stood outside the room and listened, not wanting to interrupt. But he stopped playing.

"Oh, Kenneth, that was so beautiful. I wish I could play like that," said a female voice.

"You will. I could tell the first day I heard you play. You've got what it takes."

"Do you really think so?" she laughed.

"I know so," he said.

I peeked through the small window as he reached out and grabbed the small, pretty blonde pianist around the waist. I left.

I was not mad. I did not blame him a bit. I was glad for him, in fact. I hoped that he had found someone to share his dreams and gifts with who would not throw it all away. I hoped that they would be happy and successful. The contempt that grew like a cancer to the center of my being was for myself, and for my father who had told me I couldn't make it—and had been right.

I packed, shoving only those things that I had brought from Arcata into my suitcase and trunk. Everything I had bought since being with Kenneth I left behind. All that we had collected together or he had given me as a gift stayed. Except my cello. I needed it.

At first, I thought I would go home. I didn't know what else to do. But the more I thought of facing my parents, the more I realized that I could not go there. The panic started to overwhelm me. I had to pull over.

"What do I do?" I screamed to the roof of my Buick. "I don't know what to do."

Kenneth was gone. Home was gone. The person I always wanted to be was gone. I had no choice but to start again. I had to forget about all of it ... Jake, Mom and Dad, Kenneth, the baby, my music—me. It was either forget it all or kill myself. I did not have the courage to kill myself, so I had to figure out how to forget myself.

I don't know how long I stayed there on the side of the road. Hours I suppose. Eventually, I sat up and drove toward the ocean. I got gas and a soda. I grabbed an apartment guide and a newspaper to see the prices of housing in the San Francisco area. At a phone booth, I checked the Yellow Pages and followed the directions to a part of town I'm sure I shouldn't have been in. I found what I was looking for, opened the trunk, and took out the cello Kenneth had given me less than a year before.

I left the Cash-n-Hand Pawnshop with enough money for a deposit on a place to stay, some new clothes, and a haircut.

Part Three

October 1

Dear Me,

Have you ever seen one of those movies where someone is in the witness protection program? The heroine (it's always a woman, isn't it?) has been persuaded to testify against some drug-dealing thugs or gangster types, but she has to assume a whole new identity to protect herself from their evil wrath. That's kind of what I did. I'm not sure who I was hiding from, exactly. Myself, I guess. I got a really short, boyish haircut. I bought blue jeans and trendy T-shirts, ditched all my proper skirts and blouses, and got an extra earring pierced in my right earlobe. I didn't recognize myself. I didn't want to.

SWF-student. Seeking same to share a two-bedroom house on 19th Avenue. Must be nonsmoker, easygoing, cat lover. Call for appointment.

So I did. I made an appointment to meet this SWF at

eleven o'clock on Saturday. Her name was Catherine Smith. Two years earlier, she had inherited a house from her aunt with a pink facade and one-car garage that was filled with exercise equipment. She studied communications at San Francisco State, which was within easy walking distance. But in reality, it didn't matter what her transcript said. Her purpose for attending college was abundantly clear: P-A-R-T-Y.

She opened the door wearing a T-shirt that barely covered the necessities, eating a piece of apple pie with her hands.

"Come on in," she said. A piece of crust flew out of her mouth. "Excuse the mess. I don't know what I was thinking scheduling you so early."

"Do you want me to come back?"

"No, it's fine with me if it's fine with you."

"Sure."

"Just give me a sec." She left down the hallway, bumping into a guy in striped boxers who had just come out of what I figured was the bathroom.

"Hey," he grunted in my direction.

I smiled.

He followed Catherine into the back bedroom.

There were bottles and half-empty glasses all over the front room. I started to fold up the crumpled blanket on the couch, until it suddenly moaned and moved and I noticed black hair on top of the throw pillow. The sleeping girl's shirt had the same Greek letters as Catherine's.

Sorority girls. Perfect.

Catherine came back wearing a different shirt and bike shorts. She'd finished her pie, except for the piece that was left on her chin, and was twisting her blonde hair into some sort of a braid.

"Sorry about that. I didn't realize how late it was until the doorbell rang. Can I get you anything?"

"No thanks."

"Well, I need some coffee, so come on in the kitchen and we'll talk."

Beer bottles and bowls of cat food covered the small kitchen. Somehow she found a clean coffee cup and offered me some again. I accepted.

"You said your name was Valerie?"

"Vanessa. Vanessa Palmer. And you're Catherine, right?"

"That's me. I'd tell you that the place usually isn't like this, but I'd be lying. I don't find time to clean much. But we have fun. Where are you from?"

"Seattle area, a small town." Sounded good.

"Never been there, but I've heard it's nice."

"Yeah, lots of rain, but it's pretty." I'd been there once when I was seven for an uncle's funeral.

"Why'd you come down here?"

"I don't know. My dad used to live here and I've always wanted to. I was getting sick of small-town life, I guess. What about you? Have you always lived here?"

"No. I grew up in Marin, but my parents split up when I was in high school and when I got sick of being their little pawn, I moved in with my great-aunt and finished high school here. She died a year ago and left me this place. But it costs a fortune just to heat it, so I thought I'd get a roommate to help out."

"Makes sense."

"Let me show you around. This is Mandy," she said, reaching down to stroke the cat that was walking circles around her feet. It was some strange Siamese, tabby mix with blue eyes and a striped tail. "She owns the place. It isn't fancy, but you can't beat the location, and I'm only asking $300 a month. I can't tell you it's quiet or calm, so if you want that you'd better not take it. But it is fun and convenient and you can do pretty much whatever you want. Believe me, it beats the dorms. I have friends who live there, and they can't even bring guys into their rooms."

"I'll take it."

"Great. Why don't you come back on Monday to sign papers and stuff? My dad's a lawyer and he said he'd make a contract up for me. I'll get it tomorrow and then you can move in."

"Sounds good to me."

"Excellent."

I slept in my car for the next two nights. I called Mom on a pay phone and tried to sound as relaxed as possible.

"I just wanted to let you know that I'm moving. I won't have a phone number or anything until Monday, but I wanted you to know where I was."

"What do you mean? It's nearly the end of the semester. Where are you moving?"

"To San Francisco. A lot's been happening since I saw you last."

There was a long silence. I could hear the seagulls squawking in the distance. She must have been on the porch.

"San Francisco. Wh-wha-what things have been happening, Vanessa?" When she was frustrated, her words always got flubbed up.

Mine came out clear and easy.

"Don't get worked up, Mom. I just finally came to my senses. You guys warned me a long time ago about trying to make a living off the cello. I kept seeing people graduate from the conservatory and then have to wait tables until 'something comes along.' I just figured I could find better ways to spend my time and your money."

"You don't have to worry about the money, Ness."

"Well, anyway, the only reason I was going to UOP was for the conservatory. San Francisco State has a good business school, and it's a whole lot cheaper. Their summer courses start soon, so I'd thought I'd better get settled early. I've met some girls and we're renting a place together right next to campus. I really like the city."

The story kept flowing out of me effortlessly. I don't think I even flinched when she mentioned Kenneth.

"Is Kenneth moving to the city after graduation? Is that why you want to move?"

"No, Mom. I don't know where Kenneth is going after graduation. It doesn't really matter."

"I'm sorry, honey. I just figured. You guys seemed so close when you were here ..."

"Well, you know what they say about college romances. They change as often as a freshman's major." I laughed.

She tried.

"Really, Mom. It's been over a long time. I need to start getting serious about my future. I'm getting old, you know?"

"You're getting old. Oh, please."

She sounded more relaxed.

I was starting to get good at this.

"I'll call you when I get my new number, okay?"

"Okay. Take care of yourself."

I intended to. But my first goal was to start making some of the stories I had made up happen for real.

I moved into Catherine's house with one suitcase, a trunk, and a few bags of my new clothes. I felt detached, like I was in a movie that was being written as it went along. Any good actor needs motivation to become a convincing character. My motivation was to cover up the dark pain that permeated every part of the "real me," a pain that I did not understand and refused to examine. Like putting a Band-Aid where stitches are needed, I stopped the bleeding, but the wound never healed.

I registered in the business school. I found the courses boring and useless, perfect for the new me. I worked in the research area of the library. I filed books and typed reference guides into the computer system, mindless work for someone who didn't want to use her mind. And when I was not at school, I was drinking. For "when in

Rome, do as the Romans do." Only in this case, I was hanging with the Greeks.

I did not join Catherine's sorority. I was an honorary member of sorts. They drank for a sadistic sort of entertainment. They'd drink until they were excessively happy, kept drinking until they were excessively sad, drank a little more until they were sick, and then passed out on the bed, couch, or floor.

I drank out of need. One beer (or wine cooler or rum and Coke) would help me talk. Two would help me smile. Three, to laugh. After that, I could forget that I was someone who killed her baby to keep a boyfriend who left her anyway. And if I was lucky, I could numb things enough, without vomiting, to pass out and sleep a dreamless sleep.

Unfortunately, I kept waking up. And I'd find that I needed two drinks to talk, three to smile ... and more and more to stop the dreams.

October 2

Dear Me,

It's amazing how clearly I remember this portion of my life. It would be nice if all the brain cells I killed with booze would be the ones that held the memories of how stupid I acted while drinking, but no such luck. I remember most of what I did while drunk and most of what I did when I added sex to my stock of coping mechanisms.

It started in February. Valentine's Day, I think—isn't that sweet. "Let's go skiing," said Catherine to the group of us nursing coffee cups and watching *Scooby Doo*.

"Okay," we all said. Why not?

Catherine's lawyer daddy had bought her a Bronco to make her mom feel guilty for the mere diamond studs she had given Catherine for her birthday. "There's an upside to irreconcilable differences," she told me. We filled it up with duffel bags, parkas, skis, if we had them, and a liquor store's worth of libations. Only the necessities.

I had only skied twice before. With Kenneth. I had mastered the snow plow under his patient tutelage. Two of my companions were much better than me, Catherine was worse, but it did not matter because by the time we were up on the slopes, we were so inebriated we all looked like a bunch of fools.

"Here, have an orange," Jason said when we got into the tram. (Did I mention their names? Jason, Chris, Debbie, Jon, and Catherine. See, I remember it all!)

I was freezing and would have preferred a hot chocolate with peppermint schnapps. But I ate the orange. Jason and Chris laughed when I bit into the first section. They had injected the fruit with vodka, an old fraternity trick.

"Screwdrivers-to-go," they yelled in unison. I ate two on the ride up. I got my hot chocolate with schnapps after lunch in the lodge. By two o'clock (well before then, I'm sure), I had no business placing two sticks on my feet and tearing down the side of a mountain.

"Come on, Vanessa, let's take a shortcut," said Jason.

I followed him through the trees into progressively deeper powder. He went whooping and hollering over stumps and between the trees. This far off the bunny slopes, my private lessons were failing me, and soon I could no longer see his red parka through the trees.

The slower I went, the deeper my skis became buried in the loose snow. Like a car spinning its wheels in the mud, soon I was thigh deep and stuck. Inexperience and alcohol made me unable to focus on the problem. At first, I laughed. I had to go to the bathroom, and I was wondering how I was going to make it to the lodge without making some yellow snow. I kept trying to move my feet forward, but I just kept going deeper. I was cold and I was getting tired. It started to snow. I started to panic.

Then I lay down.

It was probably the stupidest thing I could have done, allowing my whole body to get wet and colder, and the snow was really coming down. But I didn't know what else to do. I wanted to sleep. I thought maybe this time I would really not wake up. I closed my eyes and drifted into the cold darkness. I don't know how long I was there. Then I heard my name.

"Vanessa! Vanessa, where'd you go? Vanessa!"

I didn't call out. I tried to push myself deeper in the snow.

"Vanessa! Vanessa!"

He found me.

"Come on, Vanessa, get up, are you okay, what's hurt, get up, Vanessa, get up," said Jason. The poor guy was all freaked out. "I'm so sorry. I thought you were right behind me. Did you hit a tree or something? Let's get you to First Aid."

"No, no. I'm fine, really. Just help me up. I got in so deep, I couldn't get out."

"Oh, God, I'm so sorry." He put his arms around me and helped me up.

His arms felt good and warm. His eyes looked really concerned. It felt better than trying to bury myself in the snow. "Do you have any more of those oranges?" I asked, because I couldn't think of anything else to say.

He laughed and kissed me for longer than I think he expected. "You lush, let's get you warmed up." We did. We didn't ski again for the rest of the trip.

He was the first of many guys that I'm too ashamed of and see no need to mention. It reminds me of when I was young (younger) and lactose intolerant. The height of my rebellion back then was sneaking the half-gallon of chocolate or, even better, chocolate-chip mint ice cream up to my bedroom. I'd eat the whole thing. About a half an hour after the binge, I'd be in the bathroom, on my knees, depositing green and brown-flecked vomit into the pale yellow bowl. I'd go to bed with a headache and stomach cramps and swear that I would never do it again. But sure enough, a few weeks later, when nothing else seemed capable of squelching the craving, I'd sneak back upstairs with my spoon and cardboard container. I don't know why I didn't stop; it just tasted so good.

I found that when I felt lonely and depressed and totally unlovable, which was whenever I was sober, I could numb my common sense with alcohol and indulge my craving for affection with sex. There was always a willing body at the end of a party who would claim love and devotion to anyone who would allow him to stay the night. And it would feel good. When you're drunk, you believe anything. I let myself believe that I meant something to the guys. I let them love me, use me, share every part of me ... physically. Sometimes they even stayed around for a few weeks. But they would always leave, having received what they wanted and knowing that there was always more waiting at the next party. And I would be left lonelier than ever, and needing another drink. I kept telling myself to stop it. It wasn't worth it. But as soon as someone looked at me twice, asked me to dance, to stay—I'd let him in, craving for love that would stick.

Of course, none of them did. But I kept grabbing my spoon. You'd think I'd get tired of throwing up.

October 3

Dear Me,

One did stick for a while. Jamie was his name. He kept trying to be nice to me. He took me to dinner, I mean, like pasta and red wine, not pizza and beer. He wanted to know about my past, what I wanted out of life ... he made me nervous. I had to keep my altered reality straight, which wasn't easy since I was half-drunk part of the time and completely drunk the rest. I wanted him to know me. But at the same time, I was too scared to let him get close. I began laying bricks between us, trying to keep him with me, but at a distance. He put up with it for several months. I don't know why. But finally, I managed to build a wall thick enough to keep him away for good.

I suppose that event is what led to my final plunge. Halfway through the spring semester, I was missing too many classes to keep up. I dropped out. Student employment was for students, so I lost my job at the library. I lived on my savings for a month or so, until Spring Break came along. By this time, I wasn't sleeping at all, only tossing and turning through alcohol-induced nightmares that were getting more graphic and disturbing. I needed money and had no idea how to get it. So I drank a little more. Perfectly logical, don't you think?

Catherine had a big "Spring Break Kick-off" party at the house. In familiar fashion, hordes of college coeds came to get drunk before heading down to Palm Springs for the week. I wasn't going to Palm Springs, but I went ahead and got drunk anyway. But strangely, I did not find peace in the mind-numbing alcohol. The more I drank, the more restless and depressed I became. I started to panic about my money problems. I kept picking up the phone to call my parents to ask for help, but I knew I wouldn't be able to keep it together on the phone. So I came up with a really brilliant idea: I'd drive home and talk to them in person. I was so drunk I was afraid to use the phone, but it didn't even phase me to get behind the wheel of a car. Brilliant.

God was definitely with me. He had to have been. If I'd been alone, there would have been at least five more obituaries in the following week's paper.

I left the house around nine, heading toward Highway 1 and the long, winding, treacherous cliffside road home. I alternated between crying hysterically and sadistically laughing at the mess I had made of my life. I tried to work out how I would approach my parents for some extra cash. I decided that if Dad questioned my worthiness of a hand-out, I'd let him know what I really felt about him. How I knew he never loved me and wished that I had died instead of Jake. How he was a useless father, and that the least he could do was give me a few dollars. I would promise him that in exchange for his "generosity," he would never have to see me again. Brave thoughts.

Somewhere around Duncan's Mill, the sleep that eluded me back in San Francisco began to creep over me. I rolled down the window to let the cool ocean air in, and turned up the music—loud.

The last thing I remember, before waking up in the back of a Sonoma County Police cruiser, was the mournful voice of Sting, wailing, "Every breath you take, every move you make ... I'll be watching you." No joke.

Somebody was.

I had fallen asleep, or passed out, while trying to maneuver a sharp curve in the road. Swerving into the wrong lane, I narrowly missed a van carrying a mom and dad and their two sleeping children. They ended up in a ditch on my side of the road, and I crashed into the barrier designed to keep wayward cars from plunging into the Pacific Ocean. My mammoth Buick saved me from serious injuries, aside from a nasty cut on the forehead and a concussion. The family was minus an axle, but otherwise unharmed.

It was completely dark, aside from the flashing lights of the cruiser. As it drove away, the red-blue-white face of the father, holding his crying, cold daughter, staring at the delinquent who had nearly killed them, was indelibly emblazoned upon my mind. I saw the face of my mother screaming, clutching Jake's baseball cap. I saw my father drinking in his study, crying when he thought no one could hear him. I could have been the demon in that family's life. Somehow I had been spared, and I knew I was unworthy of the favor.

October 4

Dear Me,

Though I didn't realize it for a long time, my little stint in the slammer was a defining moment in my life. Maybe not on the scale of Jake's death, but still very significant. I'd always considered it one of those, "Oh yeah, by the way, I went to jail once ... isn't that a hoot!" kind of things. The reality of the experience was really easy to block out of my memory bank because of the sheer humiliation of it all. Yet, looking back now, I realize that it was so much more than that. Surrounded by grimy gray walls, filthy toilets, and people I had been taught to avoid on the street, I was pointed in the general direction of the winding path to healing. In any case—I got my act together after jail. Don't get me wrong—I had a whole lot of stupid left up my sleeve. But I learned to be stupid without being drunk, and that was a step in the right direction.

Jail is just as bad as they show it in the movies. But you can't smell it in the movies, and that's the worst part. All sorts of unsavory aromas that I could not determine if I wanted to—which I don't, believe me—mixed together in a small place with no ventilation. I vomited. Which, of course, just made it worse. People were mean, nasty, crude, and dirty. And they smelled bad. I guess I was lucky to be as drunk as I was, because I did manage to sleep at some point during the night. Can you smell in your sleep? I'm sure I did.

I went before the judge the next morning. He was nice. I suppose he saw that I wasn't a killer, just a stupid kid with a problem. He fined me $500, restricted my license, and impounded my car. I had to attend DUI education courses and AA meetings. "Don't make me regret this, Miss Palmer. It will be jail time if there's ever a next time. Do you understand?" "Yes sir, no sir, I promise sir." I let them keep my car to pay the fine and took a bus back to San Francisco.

The gang was still in Palm Springs, so I had a couple of days of quiet. I called Mom and Dad and asked them for money. They agreed without any questions. I think it was easier for them just to send it than to ask how I was doing and why I was out of funds already. Hear no evil, see no evil, speak no evil ... everything is just fine and dandy. Redefining reality must be a Palmer trait. I was grateful. I wasn't ready to talk. I looked in the phone book for a list of local AA meeting sites and found one within walking distance. I went my first night home.

The meetings were pretty much what I expected. "Hi, I'm Bob, and I'm an alcoholic. I've been coming to these meetings for three years and I've been completely sober for twenty-six months." Applause and several affirmations of "well done, brother" emerged from the folding metal chairs. "Let's recite the Twelve Steps to Recovery. If you are new, they can be found on the first page of your notebook. 'We have admitted we are powerless over alcohol, our lives have become unmanageable. We have come to believe that a power higher than ourselves ...'" We droned on and on, street bums and businessmen alike, as though we were at Sunday Mass.

When it was all over, most of the attendees gathered around the back table for weak coffee and store-bought cookies. I didn't want either, so I walked home and had only one beer before bed.

I went back every night, like a good little convicted drunk driver, but it wasn't until the second full week that I started thinking about what we recited every night. "A higher power" greater than myself—what a concept. The attendees who had found victory over alcohol did so by grabbing on to their "higher power" and using it to get them out of their messed-up lives. Bingo. That's what I needed. I didn't really want to drink. Thankfully, I wasn't physically addicted to the stuff. It was the mind-numbing and life-avoiding properties of it that I liked. I decided that if I found something to hang onto that could help me to cope with all the garbage of my life, I wouldn't need to drink at all. I pondered this concept constantly.

Meanwhile, my degenerate roommates were sabotaging all my good intentions. The two worlds did not mesh.

"If you were a recovering gambling addict, would you take your summer vacation in Las Vegas? Would you buy *Playboy* magazines, just for the insightful articles, if you were a recovering porn addict? No, I don't think so. Then why would a recovering alcoholic hang out at a bar or live with another alcoholic who is not ready to be helped?" asked Bob at my next meeting.

That was the motivation—the proverbial kick in the butt—that got me to move out and move on in search of my higher power.

October 5

Dear Me,

The next day, I took the bull by the horns. There had only been a stale bagel and a too-brown banana at the house, so I took a bus into Union Square to get a muffin and some books. I wanted to look into all my religious options before I chose which power I'd turn to. I strolled up and down the streets, listening to the street musicians. It was by chance that I spotted The Book and Brew on my way to Waldenbooks. It was sandwiched between a restaurant and small Chinese pharmacy. I had probably walked by it a dozen times before without giving it second thought. It looked like the perfect funky-hippie-used-book type of a store that would have good coffee and lots of spiritual books. It was.

The ceiling was painted as a sort of New Age Sistine Chapel—disciples around the table resembling flower children and a character who appeared like Jesus, but upon closer examination was decidedly female, with cleavage and curves coming out of her pastel robe.

The books were stored in individual, painted shelves. The science and nature shelf was decorated with animals of the sea, land, and air on one half and the solar system on the other. The children's section had small shelves decorated with teddy bears and blocks and baby dolls. The cooking section was covered with pasta and pans and vegetables of all colors, so when you took down the *Joy of Cooking* you might uncover a chunk of cheddar or bright green pear. It was truly brilliant.

The coffee bar was my favorite. The bar itself was painted like a china cabinet with glass windows and ornate handles. The high-backed chairs in front of the bar and around the small tables looked like hand-painted china teacups, while the tables looked like saucers.

I wanted to stay there forever, just to look at the artwork. I ordered a pumpkin muffin and cappuccino.

Loud voices interrupted the peaceful ocean sounds that floated out of the speakers mounted high on the shelves, painted as if you were seeing inside of them.

"So that's it, Deirdre? You're just going to leave?" the guy running the register asked the tall, overly-pierced waitress.

"I gotta, Jeffrey. It's time to move on. I'm sorry. It's been great, for both of us."

"No notice or anything? That's what I get for giving you a place to live and a job when you needed it most?" Jeffrey was getting mad. Everyone in the store stopped and stared.

"Like I didn't give you anything you needed?" The girl laughed, shaking her head. She had this amazingly thick plaited hair that bounced across her shoulders like a horse's tail shooing flies.

"Well, fine then. Go."

"I can't ignore the signs, Jeffrey. It's time for me to go. Don't be mad." She walked over, kissed him, and left—shooing flies all the way out the door.

Jeffrey rubbed his sand-colored mustache with the back of his thumb, shrugged his shoulders, and shouted out, "Does anyone need a job?"

Before I had time to think, I raised my hand like a schoolgirl and said, "I do."

"Cool. When can you start?" Jeffrey asked with a smile.

"Now."

"Cool."

Who takes a job like that? I even ended up moving into the apartment on the second level of the bookstore on that same day. Like I said before, I had a whole lot of stupid left up my sleeve.

October 6

Dear Me,

The Book and Brew, or "B & B," as I liked to call it, was—how should I say it—unique. To understand the place, you have to understand Jeffrey a bit. Jeffrey Griswold, the guy who hired me, turned out to be the artist/owner/proprietor of the shop. He had inherited it from his grandfather, Gregory Griswold, a poet and songwriter of the '50s and '60s who had become a local legend in his own right to the "alternative culture" crowd that still inhabits much of the San Francisco Bay area. He had lived in this building with several other "followers" for years. The colorful, animal-like masks that lined the stairwell and that marked the bathroom doors were Gregory's work. Underneath each mask was a small plaque with an excerpt from one of his poems or songs. My favorite was a half-lion and half-Martin Luther King, Jr. that read, "Power, like peace, can only be found in the depths of the eternal soul."

Jeffrey had lived in the store for five years. He was obsessed with it. When he was not helping customers find the perfect book for growing herb gardens in window boxes, he was painting or repainting sections of the walls in his "studio." Most of the time, he was one of those peace-love-and-happiness guys, unless his work was not progressing well. Then he was the one person on earth you avoided like the plague.

There were two other employees/housemates of the B & B. Brian, the "Brew guru," ran the coffee bar with all the wit and good-heartedness of a bartender. And then there was Alice. She handled the money. Bookkeeping, ordering, payroll—stuff like that. I'll get to her more, later. I have to, I know. God knows I'd rather keep that whole epic adventure locked away deep down in the nooks and crannies of my brain. But Doug would not allow that, now would he?

My role at the B & B? I was the waitress-cashier-whatever-else-needed-to-be-done girl. I took orders and delivered steaming, salad-bowl-sized cups of coffee or cappuccino to the patrons who sat at the teacup tables or lounged in the mismatched chairs scattered around the store. I shelved books, climbed up ladders to retrieve those hard-to-reach must-haves, and I told Alice when a customer had requested an item we did not have. Alice was our book buyer. And she went about this part of her job with the fervor of a gold miner.

I remember the first time I accompanied her on a hunt.

"Look, can you believe it? They're getting rid of a second-edition collection of Emerson for twenty-five cents. What morons."

"Yeah, morons." I didn't really know if I'd have asked a nickel, but I didn't say so.

"Do you read much?" she asked as we looked among the tables for more treasures.

"No, not really. My mom teaches college literature. I guess it's kind of like having a mom who cooks really well. What's the point of learning, since she handles it so well herself? I never got into the habit, I guess." I remember feeling very strange about pouring that much real information about my family into one sentence. I had spent so long making up a life, my honest-to-goodness information felt like a lie.

"Well, we'll have to change that. We all read anything

and everything. It's a great way to open your mind to the world around you."

"I'm sure you're right. Who's 'we'?" I asked.

"The housemates. Jeffrey, Brian, and I, and now you. It's kind of a requirement. We rotate cooking, Saturday-morning shop openings, and the latest literary masterpieces."

"Well, then I guess now's as good a time as any to start, huh?" I said.

"Sure. You'll love it. It really frees you."

Sounded good to me.

Part Four

October 8

Dear Me,

Is it okay to have fond memories from a period of your life that was totally wrong? Should I look back at this time and be disgusted and appalled by everything? I am embarrassed and confused by it, no doubt. But it was a good time—if you can rate something as "good" totally based on feelings. In fact, it is one of the only times I would classify as fun or enjoyable over this entire history of mine. Things were peaceful and crazy and spontaneous. I had no need for alcohol or sex or anything. We all just lived.

Brian was the crazy one. He'd come up with the greatest ideas. One night, close to Halloween, he came in with armloads of clothing from the Goodwill store. He had collected costumes for us to dress up like gangsters and stage a shoot-out on Halloween night. Dressed in pinstripe suits and boilers, red flapper-like dresses and garter belts, we staged a scene right out of the 1930s. Business was hopping that night. As were most.

I even got used to Jeffrey's idiosyncrasies. He had many personalities, not unlike the many masks and diverse artwork all around the B & B. He was a level-headed problem-solver one moment and an egocentric, self-absorbed artist the next. He'd yell at me one moment for interrupting his "creative process" and then slap me playfully on the rear, whistling "I'm a Yankee Doodle Dandy" with carrot juice in his mustache the next.

We'd close the shop early, order take-out sushi, and sit on the floor listening to Japanese mystic music until midnight. We gathered books by the carload and delivered them to homeless shelters or on the streets of Haight Ashbury. They probably would have been better off with a bowl of chicken soup and some blankets, but we felt good about what we did. Once, we opened the shop on a Saturday for inner-city school children and their parents. We helped them pick out books and gave them muffins and hot chocolate. It felt good, right, worthy.

It was a "spiritual" place, to find no better word to describe it. We didn't go to church. That was entirely too stifling for us. But we were each searching for something to believe in. We read about Eastern religions and mysticism. Jeffrey started dating what I now realize was a witch and got into some weird voodoo-type stuff. It didn't last long. Nothing did with him. I can't remember what he got into next. He was too hard to pin down, but he always had a plethora of interesting doctrines to discuss.

Brian was a backslidden Jehovah's Witness. He didn't like the strict regulations but wanted something to fall back on during religious debates. I kind of stayed away from it with him. I knew I would never be good enough to be one of the blessed 144,000, and I doubted he would be either, so what was the point of arguing?

Of the whole group, Alice had it the most together. She exuded peacefulness and joy, and I totally idolized her. She was not beautiful by the world's standards. My mother would have called her hefty. Her watch and crystal rings looked like they had grown out of, rather than been placed on, her arm and fingers. She had wild, kinky-curly hair and her eyes were too small for her face. But she was beautiful beyond words in my eyes. I was determined to learn her secret. I pursued her. Like a star-struck teenager meeting her idol from Hunk magazine, I followed her around and asked her questions constantly. I wanted to be just like her when I grew up.

"How can you stay so even-tempered all the time, Alice? Nothing ever bothers you," I said one night after one too many espressos.

"Oh, I haven't always been so easygoing. I fought my life for years," she said.

"How so?"

"I was born in Iowa, of all places, and knew I wanted out before I knew there were other places to go. My dad was a farmer and my mom was a housewife. My brother grew up to be a farmer and my sister grew up to be a farmer's wife. I just wanted to leave. My dad always called me the black sheep, but I think I was more like a purple one. I was totally out of place."

"I think I know what you mean," I said. "How did you get out?"

"Well, I got caught having a roll in the hay, quite literally, with the boy next door. I was sixteen. I had learned early on that boys were willing to love me, unlike my daddy, even if it was only for a few short moments out in the barn. Dad picked me up and slapped me upside the head. The poor boy got thrown against the wall and got a nasty black eye. I took my meager savings and bought a Greyhound ticket west and south and worked my way down to San Francisco. I've never heard from my family since."

"Do you miss them?"

"Yes and no. I do wonder how they are. I guess I could call, but I don't know what I'd say after all this time. They have their life, and I have mine. It's not their fault that I was so different. Who can answer the 'whys' of families? We are all made from a man and a woman. We don't choose them, and they don't choose us. The Divine Creator is in charge of that. We just move along and become who we are meant to be. I am fine with where I am and who I am. And if one day my path leads me back to them, then so be it. I will cross that bridge if it comes. Why worry? It's so unproductive."

"Yeah, but how do you stop from worrying?"

Sitting around a green Formica table eating Rocky Road ice cream, Alice began to open my eyes to what made her different. She began to share with me her religion, her philosophy of life that made her at peace with herself and the world around her. I was hungry. I accepted. For better or for worse.

October 12

Dear Me,

I AM NOT A LESBIAN! I just had to get that out of my system. I've always believed you either are or you aren't; you don't control it or choose it for a spell. But this spell of mine has always confused me. In fact, I had to have a phone session with good old Doug to get me willing to put the pen back to paper. He said I couldn't skip it.

"Why do you think this bothers you so much? You've already uncovered lots of pretty uncomfortable things here."

"I don't know."

"'I don't know' has got no wings; it won't fly in here. You know that," he said in his best counselor's voice.

"I know. I know. But I can't figure this one out."

"Yes you can."

"How?"

"What scares you about it?"

"I guess. Well. It's like ..." (spit it out, Vanessa) "I

wonder since I did it for a while, maybe I really am a lesbian deep down inside."

"What makes someone a lesbian?"

"I used to think that you were born that way. Like a gene or something."

"And now?"

"There's obviously choice involved."

"Why?"

"Because I had a choice. I chose it for a while, then it unchose me."

"I see. You didn't unchoose it?"

"No. She dumped me."

"That bothers you, doesn't it?"

"I guess it does."

"You could have found another lesbian lover. Why didn't you?"

"I didn't want one."

"Why not?"

"Because I wanted Alice."

"Why?"

"She was so ... I don't know ... peaceful. So right with the world."

"So it wasn't necessarily her physical love that you were attracted to, but her 'rightness'?"

"Yeah."

"Were you in love with Alice like you love Dale, now?"

"No. I loved who I thought she was."

"So, are you a lesbian?"

"No."

"Can you talk about it better now?"

"Yes, I think so."

"Then I'll see you next week. Okay?"

"Thank you, Doug."

"Hey, it's a tough job, but somebody's got to do it."

It all boils down to this: I was looking for someone to believe in. I needed security, strength, and warm-fuzzy love to keep me sober and to shield me from the shame that I didn't want to face. I found it all in Alice.

She called herself enlightened. She combined parts of Eastern religion and philosophy with Western Christianity into an attractive belief system. She believed that we are unable to find answers for life's problems outside of ourselves. Instead, by focusing our attention away from the hindrances of the world and toward our Higher Self, we become one with GOD and able to focus all His power through our lives. In essence, we all were capable of oneness with the world and GOD itself, by discipline and visualization.

Of all I had heard about religion before, this was the most freeing. Of everything I had seen of religion before, Alice was the greatest example of living out what she believed. There was no need to follow a set of rules, no rituals to perform, or confessionals to attend. Instead, you looked to yourself. Nothing was bad in and of itself, only the way you responded to it. My only problem was that I still couldn't see anything good in the self to whom I was supposed to turn.

Alice helped me to find that too.

We spent hours together. Restocking shelves,

searching for treasures in garage sales. Alice showed me what it was like to be loved and love without restrictions.

"You worry too much about what people think of you, Vanessa," she said one day when I was sulking over one of Jeffrey's scoldings. "You can't let his words affect how you see yourself. You are perfect in and of yourself, despite what he says."

"How do I do that? Just ignore him?"

"Well, not exactly. You rechannel the negative energy from him, out of your consciousness and toward something outside of you that is bad."

"I don't get it."

"Well, if you let all the negative karma that circles around you enter into your being, it will invade you like a cancer and eat away at the joy that is rightfully yours."

"How do you avoid it?"

"Visualize. Whenever I experience a negative situation or thought, I simply picture in my mind the most horrifying, ugly thing I can imagine. Like the Holocaust, or the KKK, prejudice, intolerance, anything that is really bad. Then I visualize the negative feelings or words, how they make me feel, and I give them to the thing that is already bad. I pretend I'm giving it a present of filth, to add to its collection and get it out of my sight."

"Isn't that kind of like feeding the fire of hatred or something?" I asked.

"No, because it is already bad. It will always be bad. It's like adding black paint to black paint trying to make it blacker. All you get is black, right?"

"Yeah, I guess so. How do you choose what to give it to?"

"It changes sometimes, depending on what I've seen or read about. I just take the first thing that comes to my mind when I think of something bad and I give it my negative 'gift.' And I don't ever take it back. Try it."

I closed my eyes and tried to picture the first thing that came to mind when I thought of bad and hurtful. I saw my father. I tried to see something else, but he kept sitting there in my mind shaking his head at me. I handed over my gift—all the hurt feelings and negative thoughts—wrapped in black paper with a black ribbon, and I left it there. I immediately felt better.

Late into the night, Alice would share with me her methods of attaining freedom from worldly bondage. She would lead me through visualization exercises, meant to get us in touch with our inner self, our God-being within us. She taught me about getting rid of my ego and allowing my spirit-nature to take control. I was really getting into it, until we hit a roadblock in my journey to enlightenment. Dream interpretations. She believed that our dreams were messages from our spirit-self, wanting to connect with our waking bodies. She wanted me to share my dreams with her.

I couldn't. I was gaining freedom in my life through her teachings during the day, but my nights were still haunted by the recurring dream of my shattered baby on the porch. It didn't matter what I did, the dream continued. I could not bring myself to tell her about it.

Every morning she'd ask what I dreamt about. I lied

about them for months. Then I would give all the negative feelings of guilt that I'd experience after lying over to my dad, who was gaining quite a collection of black boxes. I felt more at peace than ever, but the one blemish in the perfect religion I was creating tormented me. And since dreams, according to Alice, were an expression of my deepest spiritual self, I felt like there was something grossly wrong with me, that I was somehow spiritually defective. Until she broke through.

"You're holding something back, Vanessa," Alice said during one of our visualization sessions. "What is it that you see? Past your surroundings, deep in the center of you, what do you see?"

"A man." Kenneth.

"Who is he?"

"An old boyfriend."

"What is his name?"

"Kenneth."

"What do you feel when you see him?"

"Pain. Hurt."

"Why?"

"Because I loved him."

"That isn't painful."

"It ended up painful."

"Why?"

"I couldn't keep it."

"Keep what?"

"His love."

"Was it yours to keep?"

"I thought it was."

"But was it?"

"I guess not."

"So why does it hurt?"

"Because I wanted it, and when it was gone, I realized how much I'd lost."

"What did you lose?"

"A lot."

"Nothing he could do takes away the good in you. Do you believe that?"

"No."

"How could he take away your goodness?"

"I only felt good when I was around him, so I did things to keep him around. And he left anyway. I guess I feel he took everything good with him."

"But the good is who you are. There is nothing worth having or looking for outside of yourself. What you are looking for does not come from anyone or anything outside of you. Within you is a treasure far beyond any gold or love or passion. It is the indwelling god, the lordhead in you, that is you and you are it. Your worth is inside. Not in Kenneth, or anyone else. It is who you are." She moved over and wrapped her arms around me.

I cried.

"Let go of it, Vanessa. Whatever is holding you back, let go of it. Get it out of you. Only then will you be free."

"I can't. I can't say it."

"Yes you can. It is not you. It can never be you."

"I killed my baby."

I waited for her to drop her arms from me. To gasp and shake her head in disgust. She just kept holding me.

"Why?"

"I wasn't supposed to get pregnant. It messed up all of our plans. He said it would be better, it would take care of everything. I wanted to believe him. I wanted to be with him forever. So I did it, and he left me anyway. How could I have done it?"

"Because you loved him and thought that he was the most important thing about you. He wasn't. You are the most important thing."

"But I killed my baby. I was so selfish."

"No you didn't. You followed what you thought was right. You did it for pure reasons. You released a soul before it was ever damaged by the world into god-consciousness. That is the most unselfish thing you could have done."

I looked up at her.

"You were not being mean or hateful. You wanted what was best for you and the one you loved. What would have been the benefit of bringing a child into a world where his or her parents were not ready to take on the responsibility? You are not bad, Vanessa. You are a perfect creation, born with god in you. Now you have to learn to appreciate who you are, despite what happened before."

"How do I let it go?"

"First, you have to let go of your bitterness toward Kenneth. He could not have made you a good person. You are good, despite any outside influence. He is a man. He is not part of your life anymore. Let it go. Let him go. Release and denounce your need for him. He is not you."

I did what she said.

"Now, you have to tell yourself over and over that you

are good, you are perfect, you are one with your creator, you are free from the hindrances of the natural world."

I did that.

"Give away all the guilt and shame and pain that you have been harboring in the deepest part of your being. Wrap it up and give it to the black place. You cannot take it back. You are full of light once the blackness is gone. You are free."

I did. And I felt free.

"You are beautiful, Vanessa. Nothing outside of you can ever change that. You are pure light." And she kissed me. Not like a friend but like someone who loved me. I kissed her back, because there was nothing outside of me or in me that was wrong. I was free.

For a while.

October 13

Dear Me,

I was deliriously happy, released from all the baggage I'd been carrying and floating in the arms of a woman and a culture that accepted me. It was exciting.

It was surprisingly easy to slip into a lifestyle that I had never considered an option before. I told myself over and over that there was nothing wrong in me; nothing outside of me could affect my life; I was the master of myself; I could do what I wanted to find happiness.

Alice made me happy. The community of women I became a part of was comforting. Wherever Alice and I went, we were met with warm smiles and knowing looks. It was like we were part of some secret organization, bonded by some unspoken sisterhood-type oath: "Having found relationships with men degrading and hurtful, I swear to find wholeness and gratification in the company of like-minded women from this day forward, so help me Goddess." It was exploration without consequences, satisfaction without guilt. Plain and simple—it was addictive.

I came to believe that men had caused all of my pain. Kenneth, my father—even Jake. It was his superiority that made me inferior in the eyes of my parents. It was his death that led me into the arms of Kenneth. He was not the perfect saint I had made him out to be. Every time I would start to feel guilty or think negatively about myself, I simply wrapped another black box and handed it to the first man that entered my mind. Dad got the most, but I did share the wealth of my bad karma with others from time to time.

Alice and her friends taught me all kinds of handy tricks to keep myself "at peace with the world." We would lie on the floor, breathe deeply, and visualize a golden ball of light that grew bigger with each breath. Its light would enter through our heads and infuse our bodies with goodness. The rays from the light met with the rays from the others and we would be bound in universal goodwill toward all. Mumbo jumbo? Yeah—but powerful mumbo jumbo nonetheless. Frighteningly powerful. It worked for me. I needed it. I needed Alice and her community of free-spirited friends. When I was with them, I felt good. When I followed their religion, I felt powerful. When I slept with Alice, I felt safe. I didn't have my dream. That alone was enough for me. I won't try to justify it or deny it. It was my life.

For about two years.

October 14

Dear Me,

Delusion: I had found healing and freedom from the pain and oppression of the past. *Reality:* Through my freedom-goodwill-and-New-Age religion, I had simply switched dependencies. What started with craving Dad's approval, then Kenneth's love, then alcohol's comfort, now needed Alice's spirituality. Different outlets for the same desire: acceptance and satisfaction. Alice worked the best. I really believed that I had it all figured out. I had no doubts.

When did it all start to fall apart? When did my golden light start to fade? My second summer there, after our trip to Southern California.

We had spent two weeks lounging in the sun, drinking virgin margaritas, dancing ... oh so romantic. We reluctantly returned home, only to find Jeffrey frantically pacing the floor when we walked in.

"Oh, Vanessa. I am so glad you're here." The look on his face sent my mind hurling back to the doorway of my cabin at Camp Cazadero. My chest tightened. *Nothing he can say changes who I am. I am good, I am right* ... I chanted in my mind—grabbing for my golden light.

"What's wrong?"

"Your mom has been calling all day. It's something about your dad. You need to call her right away."

"My mom?"

"You'd better call now. She sounds like a mess."

I went upstairs to the phone.

"Palmer residence, this is Jack."

"Uncle Jack? What are you doing there?" I asked. Dad's middle brother had only been to our house two or three times before, at Christmas. He and his wife and kids, whom I hadn't seen since they were babies, lived in Colorado. He was a forest ranger. "What's wrong?"

"It's your dad, Vanessa. Your mom wanted to be here when you called, but she had to get to the hospital. It doesn't look good."

"What doesn't look good? What's happened?"

"Well, you know how he's been coughing so much and losing all that weight." *No....* "Helen found him this morning on the floor of the bathroom. He was coughing up blood. She made him go to the doctor and they admitted him to the hospital right away."

"What is it? What are they saying?"

"Nothing yet. They're running all kinds of tests and X-rays. They took some fluid off his lungs. I don't want to say anything more without you talking to your mom. But I think you should get up here if you can."

"Well, I just got back from vacation. I'll have to see ..." my voice trailed off.

"Your mom really wants you here."

"Okay. I'll see what I can do."

"Call her and tell her that. It would make her feel better." He gave me the number of the hospital. I hung up and held the receiver in my hand. Home? I really didn't want to go. But somehow I knew I had to.

I called Mom and told her I'd be there the next day.

"I'm going to have to take some more time off, Jeffrey."

"Is everything okay?"

"It's my dad. He's in the hospital. I don't really know what's up, but Mom wants me to come home right away. I guess she's scared."

"Well, you've got to go. It's family."

Not really. *They* were my family. I wanted them to protest, to tell me how much I'd be missed. I wanted Alice to come with me.

"Are you going to be okay? I've been gone so long already and ..." wanting him to agree and beg me to stay.

"Sure, Misty is working out great, and she hasn't

landed any other work yet. I'm sure she'll be thrilled to stay on awhile longer."

Brian's little sister, this perfectly cute, perky strawberry blonde, was out of work and staying with her big brother for a while to get back on her feet. She had been filling in for me while I was gone. Alice said she would help her hold down things until I got back.

"Don't worry, Vanessa. I'm sure your dad will be okay. He just needs his little girl next to him," said Jeffrey.

I almost laughed.

The battery started dying on my golden globe of light.

October 16

Dear Me,

I hate hospitals. I've always hated them. When I was five, Mom took me to see a former student of hers. She had delivered a baby prematurely and Mom had offered to sit and watch the baby while the exhausted girl went home to take a shower. It took lots of convincing, but the girl finally left with promises of everything being fine and only a phone call away if the doctor had any news.

The smells made me light-headed and nauseous. Mom lifted me up to peer through the glass window at the baby born three months too soon. He was the size of a deflated football with tubes and tape covering his withered body. His arms and legs were no thicker than hot dogs, and he had bright red patches all over his gray skin. I got so upset that I kicked my mom trying to get out of her arms, and I ran to the bathroom just in time to throw up in the toilet. I was dizzy and thought for sure I would faint. Mom washed my face and put a wet rag on my neck. She asked if I wanted to see the healthy babies. I didn't. I found a couch in the maternity waiting room, with anxious grandparents and siblings. I lay on the couch and tried to sleep until the girl returned from what seemed like the longest shower in history. The baby didn't make it through the night.

I couldn't sleep that night thinking about leaving Alice. I begged her to come with me. I needed her. I couldn't do it without her. *Please!*

She told me to visualize my power and strength as a huge set of arms embracing all the dark emotions and illness of my parents, enveloping them with my light until no darkness remained.

"You don't need me. You are different now. Show them."

"Okay."

"I love you. Call me if you need to."

"Okay."

I drove straight to the hospital in Eureka.

He was in room 318. I walked down the hall trying to breathe deeply and visualize health and wellness. But when I looked in his room, the sight of his emaciated body hooked up to all sorts of IVs and oxygen tubes overwhelmed me. I was looking at death. Of that I was sure.

"Vanessa, you're here," Mom cried from the corner of the room. I was still standing in the door. "Grayson, she's here."

He turned his head and lifted an arm as far as the tubes would let him.

"Dad." It's all I could say. I'd spent so much time hating him that I didn't know how to process the pain I felt upon seeing his dying body. I just stared.

Mom pulled out her trusty tissue and hugged me. "Thank you for coming. I hope it wasn't a problem with your boss."

"No, it's fine." I didn't tell them that it was pretty easy to replace a coffee waitress. They still didn't know how little I was doing with my life.

We stood awkwardly silent for who knows how long.

"Do you want to get something to eat?" she asked. Ah—food to the rescue.

"Uh ... sure. I guess I am hungry." I wasn't, but I wanted to leave the room more than anything.

"We'll be right back, Grayson." She bent to kiss his forehead.

I forced myself to walk to his bedside and pat his blanketed leg. "We'll be back, Dad."

"I'm not going anywhere," he said. It sounded more like a gasp than words. He tried to smile but only coughed.

"What's wrong with him, Mom?" I asked after we left the room.

She started to sob. "He kept telling me I was overreacting—to leave him alone. 'I'm fine, stop nagging me.' You know your father. So I did. I never said another word. They think it's cancer, Vanessa. Cancer. The doctor is supposed to come tell us the results of all the tests in an hour or so. But I know it is. I just know it." She started to cry. I had to lead her by the hand to a table in the cafeteria. It smelled of old coffee and overcooked green beans.

Cancer? Lung cancer? I saw the pictures of withered black lungs in my high school health book. The charred sacks used to scare us out of ever smoking.

"Dad's never smoked." It's all I could think to say. "How could it be cancer?"

"I don't know how. I just know."

Black boxes. Black boxes of hate and pain and bad karma. I had sent him all those boxes, and they had infiltrated his body with black death. I gave him cancer. That thought entered my consciousness and settled in the center of my soul. No good thoughts of pure light could remove it. I had given my father cancer.

We pretended to drink our coffee and returned to room 318. The doctor was right behind us.

"Mr. and Mrs. Palmer. Ma'am. This is the part of my job I don't like," Dr. Jansen said.

"Just get on with it," Dad said, trying to sound irritated but revealing his fear instead.

"You have what we call Adenocarcinoma of the lung, and it looks like it's Stage 3."

"Out of how many stages?" asked my mother, taking the one chair in the room.

"Four. The cancer has spread to the mediastinum, the area between the lungs. The CAT scan revealed a thickened area on the outside of the chest wall, which makes us believe it is in the lymph nodes and surrounding tissue of the lungs, possibly the diaphragm. We will have to do some further surgery, decide on treatment options and such, but that can wait until you meet with the oncologist tomorrow." He went on and on. "We want to keep you at least overnight to get your pulse-oxygen level up and your cough under control. I'm sorry."

"How did this happen?" Mom asked. "He's not a smoker."

"Unfortunately, there are other less obvious causes of this particular form of cancer. Environmental factors, asbestos, secondhand smoke, genetics—they all play a part. Did your parents smoke?" Dr. Jansen asked my dad.

"My father did, but he died early."

"Cancer?"

"Lumber."

Confused look. Cleared throat. "Well, it is hard to answer why these things happen. For all the science and modern technology we have, we still don't have many of the answers." He looked stricken, as though he were responsible for the inadequacies of his profession. I felt sorry for him. How could he possibly know that it was the psychic negativism of his patient's own daughter that caused his lungs to turn black and diseased? Technology would never understand the power of hate.

"It's all that smoke you inhale in those tiny offices of yours. I've told you to make your people go outside to smoke. They'll probably all live to be a hundred," my mother cried.

"Hush, Helen. You don't know. It's going to be okay."

"We will do everything we can. Tomorrow you can meet with someone from oncology. They'll explain more about your options. You should try to get some rest."

"Yeah, right. With them coming in every thirty seconds to take my temperature."

The doctor laughed dryly. "Well, try anyway. I'll stop by in the morning to see how you're doing. And again, I'm sorry."

After a lot of pointless arguing, Dad finally convinced Mom to take me home. "I'm not going to die tonight. Go," he said. I think we both needed to get away from the hospital. So we obeyed. Neither of us could think of anything to say. We just kept shaking our heads. Mom wondered how this could be happening. I wondered how I could possibly live with myself with another death on my conscience.

It was late, and we were tired of trying to act comfortable around each other, so we went to bed soon after getting home. I fell asleep more quickly than I expected. The distant ocean sounds have always relaxed me.

The dream came back that night. Only this time, Dad was in it. I was sitting on the porch, holding the precious baby in my arms, and my dad was sitting next to me making googly eyes at him. When Kenneth started calling for me to come for him, I hesitated, but then Dad offered to hold the baby. "Let me," he said, taking the baby from my arms. As I walked toward Kenneth, he kept moving farther and farther away from me. I'd step forward one, he'd step backward two. The baby started to cry. When I turned around to see what was wrong, the house was moving farther and farther away. The cries got louder and louder and I could see my father pulling apart the baby limb by limb, laughing and googling the whole time. But it was like the land I was standing on was silly putty. Each side was stretching farther and farther apart, and I was in the middle, reaching toward both sides in vain.

I woke crying, my arms aching. I sat up and tried to meditate. I imagined the mountains and the blue skies. I chanted over and over, "I am perfect, nothing outside of me has any influence on me. God and I are one. I have all the power to bring peace to my life.... I am perfect; nothing outside of me has any influence on me...." It didn't work. All I could see was my father tearing apart my baby and black vultures, circling above, ready to devour what was left behind. I couldn't even fit all the images in a black box. I didn't know who to give it to anyway. I needed Alice.

I turned on the light and looked at my watch. 5:05 AM. I went to Dad's study and picked up the phone. My heart started racing before I began to dial. *Should I call? Will she be angry? Should I admit how weak I am? What can she do to help?* "If you're going to make a call, please hang up and try your call again."

I took a deep breath, mustered up enough positive energy from somewhere to keep from making a fool out of myself, hung up the phone, and headed downstairs for coffee.

I wasn't surprised to see that Mom was already up. I had forgotten that Uncle Jack was there, however, so a male voice in the kitchen startled me.

"Good morning."

"Oh, Vanessa. Did we wake you?"

"No, I was already awake. Got sick of staring at the ceiling."

"Hi, Vanessa. It's been forever since I've seen you. How's city life?" Uncle Jack got up and kissed me on the cheek. He looked so much like Dad.

"Okay."

"What are you doing now? Still playing that cello?"

Uncle Jack was the one brother who inherited their mother's musical flair. Or curse. He played the saxophone and pretty much anything else he picked up.

"Oh, not much. I don't have time with work and all."

"Don't work too hard. You're still young and talented. You have plenty of time for work. What are you doing now, anyway?"

"Managing a bookstore. I'm still trying to figure out what I want to do when I grow up," I laughed.

"Well, don't forget to have some fun too. Can you bring the pot here? We need a warm-up."

Mom looked horrible.

"Did you sleep at all?" I asked her.

"A little."

"No, she didn't. I heard her puttering around in here around three," said Jack.

"I slept a little, but I couldn't stand staying in bed thinking. I baked some cinnamon rolls."

Ahhh … food.

Mom was anxious to get back to the hospital and didn't eat more than a few bites. I forced down a roll and agreed with her that we should get going.

"I wish I could stay longer," said Jack, "but Michael starts football practice, and I promised Luanne I'd stain the deck before things got too busy."

"It's okay, Jack. I'm just glad you were here in town when this all happened. I don't know what we would have done without you."

"God works that way. He knows exactly what we need when we need it. I'm glad to be of help."

He got up and took his plate to the sink.

"Let's get going, Ness." Mom started toward her room.

We quickly got ready and met outside in the fog.

"Let me know what's happening, Helen. I'll do whatever I can."

"I will, Jack. And thanks again."

"Bye, Vanessa."

"See ya later." I hugged him as he got into his Ford truck.

"We'll be praying for you," he said as he drove away.

I remember wondering when he had gotten so religious.

The oncologist was already in the room when we got there.

"The treatment options are clear-cut in my opinion," said Dr. Caldwell, a young, pretty woman with short auburn hair and gold-rimmed round glasses. She looked more like a soap-opera star than an oncologist. "With Stage 3 NSCLC of the Adenocarcinoma type, we want to be as radical as possible to prolong survival at a suitable quality."

Bedside manner was not her strong suit.

"I'm scheduling surgery for tomorrow, to resection the left lobe and remove lymph nodes. That is about all we can do surgically. Then you will start a series of chemo, Velban intravenously every three to four weeks. You'll want to look into some home healthcare options."

She went on and on. I might as well have been watching a soap opera, as detached as I was from what she was saying. Mom and Dad felt the same way. I could tell by the glazed-over expressions on their faces.

"Any questions, Mr. Palmer?"

"How long?"

"Tomorrow will be the surgery, then we'll start chemo a week or so after that—"

"No. How long do I have?"

Her droning stopped.

"It really is too early to say. The five-year-disease-free rate of individuals with Stage 3 and higher Adenocarcinoma tends to range from 10 to 22 percent with the use of—"

"Cut the mumbo jumbo. Just tell me straight, doctor. How long?"

She adjusted her cute little glasses and examined his chart, as if her next line was written somewhere on the back page. "Two years. Maybe more. Maybe less."

No one said anything else. Dr. Caldwell turned and left room 318.

October 18th

Dear Me,

I stayed in Arcata for another week, helping Mom recreate room 318 at home in their bedroom, replete with an oxygen tank, nebulizer, adjustable bed to make breathing easier, and a shoebox filled with little brown medicine bottles. Dad stayed in bed for five days following his surgery but insisted on checking in at the office as soon as he was able to walk without choking. Mom was furious, but he was adamant. "I don't intend to just lie here and die, Helen. What's the point of that?"

I became restless. The dreams were as frequent and violent as ever. I was scared and exhausted and felt that if I stayed any longer, I'd lose everything. So much for the power of positive thinking. I left early on a warm Sunday morning. I managed to hug Dad, cringing at how weak he felt underneath my arms, and told him to take it easy.

"I will not. I plan to keep doing what I've always done."

"That might not be possible after your treatments start," I said.

"Hogwash."

I wasn't about to argue with him.

"Thank you for coming and staying so long, Vanessa. I'm sure your store is missing you greatly," said Mom.

"Oh, it's fine. I've got good people," I said. "They probably didn't even realize I was gone."

"It was good having you here."

"Call me and let me know how things are going. Get some help if you need it."

"We'll be fine."

Of course.

"Drive safe."

Of course.

"Bye, Vanessa."

"Bye, Mom."

I was so relieved to be leaving. I felt guilty about it, but I was desperate. I was floundering big time. I had the strangest feeling that I had been stuck in time. That the world had stopped ever since I'd arrived in Arcata, allowing me to play the part of concerned daughter in the strange melodrama of Dad's cancer, and now that I had said all my lines, I could return to my real life. What I didn't know was that the world I left behind had been playing in fast-forward.

The store was closed by the time I got home. We always closed early on Sundays, unless Jeffrey had a poetry reading or writers' group scheduled. I walked in the deserted store carrying a wooden planter box, a bag of soil, and several packs of seeds. Alice had been talking about starting a window garden in the kitchen. There was this great little nursery in Petaluma, where I had stopped for lunch, so I picked up a little present. I knew she'd be excited.

"Hello, is anyone here?" I called out. I had told Alice on the phone I'd be back for a late dinner. "Hello?"

Brian came down the stairs. "Vanessa. Hey, welcome home. How's your dad?"

"Home. He starts chemo next week."

"I'm so sorry."

"Thanks. Where is everybody?" I wanted to leave that part behind. Get on with my real life.

"Oh, Jeffrey is out with some girl from last week's book club. Alice and Misty went to Salmagundi's and a movie, I think. It's just me."

I tried not to look too disappointed. After all, how could I expect everyone to wait around for me? "Well, bummer. Will you help me with this stuff?" I was beginning to sag from the weight of the bag of soil.

"Oh, yeah. Sorry."

"When did they leave?" I asked.

"About an hour ago."

"Oh. Well, I've got to get my stuff out of Alice's car. Could you fix me a double cappuccino? I've been dying for one ever since I left."

"That's why they call me the Brew Master. Do you want any flavoring?"

"No. Straight up and strong, please."

He saluted me with his free hand and retreated behind his coffee counter. "Coming right up."

I drank three cappuccinos to keep awake until Alice came home at 2:00 AM. They walked in slowly. Alice was patting Misty on the back. It looked like she had been crying. I could hear the comforting tone of Alice's voice, the one that made me feel so much better, but I couldn't hear the words.

"Hi!" I said from the couch to the side of the door.

"Oh, Vanessa! You scared me." She put her hand to her chest. "I forgot you were coming home. When did you get in?"

"Around five. What have you all been up to?" I asked, trying to sound casual, but coming off shaky.

"We went to the movies and then got talking. I didn't realize it was so late," she said looking at her watch. "You've met Misty, right?"

"Yeah."

"Hi. Welcome back. I hope everything went okay," Misty said with a little wave.

"Well, as okay as can be."

"I'm so sorry," she said.

"Thanks."

"We've missed you," said Alice, finally coming toward me. We hugged.

I didn't want to let her go. She felt good. I pushed back all of the jealous feelings and told her how happy I was to see her.

She let go. "We'd better get to bed. Monday is here, and we haven't slept off Sunday yet."

We followed her hefty frame up the stairs.

Misty picked up a pillow and blanket from the chair

next to my bed and took her pajamas from my closet. "I hope I didn't leave things too messy," she said. "I tried to keep it like you had it."

"I'm sure it's fine."

"Good night." She retreated to the bathroom. She looked like a puppy whose bed was moved from the warm master bedroom to the cold garage. I had displaced her.

"It is good to have you back," Alice said. "It's not the same around here without you."

"It's good to be back," I said, desperate to ignore what I knew was true.

I came downstairs, groggily, around ten the next morning. I was mad I had slept so late; I wanted things to be normal. Sure enough, Misty was behind the counter, perkily serving coffee and a muffin to John, one of our regulars.

"Well, look who the cat drug in," said Jeffrey when he saw me. "Glad you could make it." He was trying to be lighthearted, but I took it seriously.

"You could have woken me up," I said.

"I figured you needed the sleep."

"Thank you, but I'm ready to get back in the swing of things." How do you say it? The tension in the room was so thick you could cut it with a knife. Actually, I think you would have needed a chainsaw. "Where's Alice?" I managed to ask.

I was looking at Jeffrey, but Misty answered, "She had a lead on an estate sale up on 19th. She'll be back around noon."

I held on for dear life. It was like blowing air into an inner tube with a hole in it. I blew and blew with all I was worth, but nothing was able to keep me afloat.

"There's never been just you and me, Vanessa. We are part of a much bigger picture," Alice said one night when I told her I missed us being alone together.

"What do you mean? We've spent so much time together." *Blow, blow!*

"I was opening your eyes to what was right there before you all the time. You just needed some guidance. You don't need me. All you need is right inside of you."

"But—I love you."

"I love you too. I love many people and many things. I don't rely on love to do anything for me, however. Only we can provide what we need to survive and be well."

"I need you."

"No you don't. The last thing I wanted was for you to become dependent on me. What I've been trying to do was get you to the point where you could stand on your own, feel good about yourself and your sexuality. To free you to do whatever you need to be fulfilled. Not to bind you to any one person or thing."

What a fool, what a fool, what a fool ...

"We can still be together, Vanessa. I will always be here. Just not here only for you. Do you understand?"

Did she understand? That's what I wanted to know. Did she understand that what I had believed in was her? She was my god. By detaching herself from me, I lost my foothold on the only reality I had allowed myself for two years. I had nothing left to hold onto. All of the guilt and pain and garbage that I had shoved away into another reality came pummeling back over me like thousands of angry rioters breaking through a police barricade. Their motivation was overwhelming. I was trampled.

Snapped, flipped out, became delusional, had a psychotic break of some sort ... I don't know what it would be called in technical terms. I went nuts.

October 20

Dear Me,

I have never liked confrontation. I did not like to argue or assert my opinion over the opinion of others. I preferred keeping quiet or trying to avoid any sort of conflict. I suppose that ignoring this stuff for nearly twenty-five years was not such a healthy thing to do. Once I started pulling on the string that loosely held my emotions at bay, it unraveled completely, with no chance of stopping until I was standing there naked and ashamed.

I threw coffee mugs onto the floor. I tore books off the shelves. I flung coffee on a newly painted wall and poured milk on the Persian rug. Quite the tantrum, wouldn't you say?

"Calm down, Vanessa. You've got to calm down," Jeffrey kept saying, holding his hands up against my ranting.

I just laughed some psycho-lady laugh.

"Come on now, Vanessa. Let's go upstairs and talk. This is not you. This is not who you are. Come on," said Alice.

Her motherly tone that usually calmed me made me even angrier. I threw a banana at her. "What do you know about who I am?" I screamed.

"If you don't calm down, I'm going to call the police. Get a hold of yourself." Jeffrey was losing patience.

More laughter. More flying fruit.

"Just leave, Vanessa. Leave, and I'll pretend this didn't happen," he said.

I ran upstairs. I knocked pictures off the walls. Squeezed toothpaste on the bathroom mirror. I ransacked Alice's things. Then I took out my suitcase from under the bed and threw in some clothes, not paying any attention to what I was packing and what I was leaving behind. Until a thought stabbed me right between the eyes. No joke. I had a piercing pain between my eyes like nothing I'd ever felt before ... followed by a thought spoken into the space left by the knife as clear as if someone was standing in front of me speaking into a microphone. "Take their pills."

I had known for a long time that my housemates' peace and goodwill toward men (or women) was not without the assistance of pharmaceutical intervention. I took a bottle of Xanax from Jeffrey's nightstand, a bottle of Zoloft from Misty's purse. Brian had a nice stash of sleeping pills (too much caffeine, I suppose) that I helped myself to. Alice was enlightened beyond the need for medication, so I stole her Benadryl for good measure, and her money. I stuffed them all into a small zippered cosmetic bag, grabbed my things, and walked out the door.

No, I didn't have anywhere to go. I didn't have a plan. I just began to walk, dragging my suitcase through the streets of San Francisco, not looking much different than your average homeless, slightly deranged street person. Perhaps I was a little too well-groomed to blend in without some notice. But after a night in Union Square, I was as grimy as the veterans were.

I suppose insanity was a good option for me. If I had stopped for a moment to consider with an ounce of clarity what I was doing, I probably would have been in danger. But they say that looking and acting confident keeps you from being targeted for assault. I was confidently deranged. Leaning against my suitcase, counting my stash of pills over and over again while considering what type of booze to swallow them with kept me from the harm of others.

I did this for three days and nights. Finally, I decided on vodka. I rented a car. I wanted to die by the ocean. I drove toward Highway 1. I passed a church, a stately Presbyterian one. The message board that sat on the small patch of grass next to the front steps of the church was missing a few letters. It said something like this: "Sunday Wors ip—11:00 AM Sunday School 10:00 AM. Join us. Jesus ... Don't leave Ear h without Him." I almost drove into a ditch looking at the sign. For some reason I can't explain, the words hit me like a brick wall. I had no choice but to stop. I pulled into the First Time Visitor parking area, crawled into the backseat with my bottle tucked under my arm, and cried until I fell asleep.

Part Five

October 25

Dear Me,

I believe in miracles. I have no choice. For the series of events that followed my departure from the B & B, though not the parting of the Red Sea, were miraculous. *Godulous*, as I like to say. There were definitely some pretty incredible things going on in the spiritual realm to have picked me up—quite literally—out of the gutter, and smacked me down in the center of His world. *Godulous* ...

I don't know how long I was in the car. Several hours, I suppose. I fell asleep with my knees crammed up against the back of the passenger seat and my head crooked on the armrest. I had a dream. A doozy of a dream that started out the same as the rest—just your everyday baby-being-torn-into-pieces-before-your-eyes dream. But somewhere between my reaching out to grab the baby and him falling apart on the porch, we were both grabbed up by the most hideous flying creatures I've ever seen. I mean, this was beyond Stephen King horror flick hideous—they were slimy, black, contorted things with green and yellow slime oozing from their pores and red fleshy something hanging from their mouths and claws. Major willy-causing creatures.

These things picked us up, the baby and me, and flew us to the ocean. I could feel the piercing of their claws into my side like a knife. They dropped us. I remember screaming and shaking my head, "No! I don't want to die! I don't want to die! I changed my mind, please don't make me die!" And all of a sudden, I was awake in the back of the car, screaming at the top of my lungs, clamoring to get out of the back door, but unable to open it because I was shaking so badly. I thought I was still falling. I finally managed to get the door open and I lunged out onto all fours. I felt a piercing pain and a cool wetness spreading underneath me. I was still screaming, waiting to die.

I heard a gentle voice in the distance coming toward me. "It's okay. Oh, Lord help her. It's okay. You're going to be okay." The voice was now beside me, also on all fours, and she lifted my head. "Dear Lord, help her. You're going to be just fine. Calm down. Hush now." I passed out.

A normal person would have called the police. A normal person would have left this deranged, smelly woman in the able hands of the authorities and gone on with her daily routine. But Ruth was not, is not, and will never be "normal." Ruth is a praying woman. In fact, she was leaving a prayer meeting when she heard the crash of my breaking vodka bottle shattering on the pavement. She ran toward, rather than away from my screams.

"What did you think when you saw me?" I asked Ruth the other night.

"Truthfully?"

"Of course."

"Well, I said to the Lord, 'Lord, this wasn't quite what I had in mind. But I'll take it.'"

"What do you mean?"

"That night, I came to the prayer meeting with three big needs heavy on my heart. First, I needed a companion to share my lonely home with. Second, Dale and I needed a hostess to get the restaurant started. And finally, Dale needed a wife. He wasn't getting any younger, you know. The sisters and I had prayed for these things earnestly. The Lord spoke to me as I was leaving the meeting that the next person I met was going to be the fulfillment of all three requests. I was tickled at the thought and was wondering where I should go to meet such a remarkable woman. Then I heard your scream. It wasn't what I had expected, but I knew that you were the one."

"Weren't you scared?"

"Of what?"

"Of me. I wasn't exactly acting sanely."

"I knew you needed help. That's all. I started praying and didn't stop."

"What did you think of me?"

"I thought you were a beautiful girl."

"Yeah, right." I had to laugh.

"No, I did. That's why I lifted your head. I looked into your eyes and I believe God showed me who you really were, underneath the dirt, blood, and stench of alcohol. You were beautiful."

"You're amazing."

"No. Only washed in His amazing grace."

No accidents.

October 26

Dear Me,

If I'm to believe the Bible is true, and I have grown to believe that more than I believe the world is round, I know that "our struggle is not against flesh and blood, but against the rulers and powers of this dark world." I have no other way to explain the things that happened next in my life. There was a struggle going on, a battle against the dark world I had been living in and the Light, God's world, which I was supposed to enter.

Ruth took me home. She gathered my things from the car and called the rental car company to pick up the red Grand Prix I had chosen to spend my last moments on earth in. I'd considered going the cheaper route, but who wants to die in a white Ford Escort? She led me up the stairs into her house. Picked glass shards out of my hands, then washed and bandaged them. She bathed me, washed my hair, put me in her own flannel nightgown, because she didn't want to invade my privacy by going through my bag. She put me into bed, in the guest room closest to her own, and left a light on in the hallway so I could find my way in the dark. She made herself vulnerable to my insanity. I don't think anyone else would have done it.

I woke up in the morning smelling freshly baked bread and coffee. Cinnamon. My hands hurt, my eyes burned, my stomach ached because it was empty, and I was scared to death. *Where on God's green earth was I?*

I quickly packed up my things, trying to piece together the foggy images of the night before. But instead of being grateful for all this mysterious savior had done for me, I tried to sneak out of the house. Ruth was sitting in a chair with a bird's-eye view of the front door.

"Not leaving without breakfast, are you?" she asked, sweet as sugar.

"Yes, no, well I ..." I stammered, stupid as mud.

"Come on in. You don't need to go yet, unless you're being missed somewhere. In which case you can call and tell them you'll be home in a bit."

"No. It's just that ..."

"It's just that you have no idea who I am or where you are or whether I've put arsenic in your coffee cup?"

"No. Well ... maybe."

"Do you think I would have cleaned you up and let you sleep in my house if I was going to hurt you? Believe me, if anyone has a reason to be scared, it's me. I don't know who you are either, so we're on even ground here. Now come have some coffee and warm toast, and then you can go on home. Okay?"

How was I to argue? "Thank you." I put my bag down by the front door.

Sanity had not quite returned to my brain yet. My mind was racing, I felt like I was going to faint, I didn't trust Ruth one iota, and I didn't even think I could carry on a rational conversation. Nevertheless, I was starving, and the homemade raisin cinnamon bread smelled delicious. I sat in this really fancy velvet chair and devoured three pieces, covered with whipped butter, and washed it down with strong coffee. I didn't say a word. Neither did Ruth. She kept reading her book—the Bible, of course. Its worn leather cover matched the fancy velvet chair.

I finished as quickly as I could and sat like a child at the dinner table. "May I please be excused, Ma'am?" She was so intently reading and her eyes were half closed. I thought that she was about to nod off. After a few uncomfortable minutes, I quietly stood up, thinking I could try sneaking out again.

"How'd you like that bread?" she asked.

"Great. Thank you." Caught.

"It's my grandmother's recipe. I've got a ton of them. Sourdough, honey wheat, sweet bread. Do you like sourdough?"

"Yeah." I kept glancing toward the door.

"I'll make some tonight; the starter's all ready. So, tell me a little about yourself."

"Ummmm ..."

"Well, at least tell me your name. I'm Ruth. Ruth Jacobson. And you are?"

"Vanessa."

"Vanessa. What a beautiful name."

"Thank you."

"Where are you from, Vanessa?"

"North. Humboldt County."

"Please sit down. There's no reason to rush off. Is there?"

"Well, I've been a big enough intrusion on your life. I should just be going."

"Nonsense. You've been no intrusion at all. Don't you know that old ladies love company? Sit. Please." She gestured toward the velvet chair that still bore the imprint of my rear end.

I sat.

"Good. Now, tell me, what had you screaming and swimming in a bottle of vodka last night, dear?"

She was so casual, like she was asking where I had found such a lovely shade of pink nail polish.

"I don't really want to talk about it." I was getting hot and felt like I was going to hyperventilate.

"Very well. There will be time for that. How about I go and fix you some bacon and eggs. You look like you could use a little protein."

"No, that's okay. I need to go."

"Nonsense. You just stay put. I'll be back in a jiffy."

Was this lady for real? Maybe she was crazy. "Oh, she was such a nice woman, always helping out around the neighborhood," the neighbors would say to the news reporters the day after they found me in the bathtub filleted by her serrated bread knife. But then again, who was I to complain? I was the one carrying around a stash of pills, planning to drive off a cliff. Worst-case scenario was that she would do for me what I had not succeeded at the day before. I leaned my head back and breathed in the scent of bacon wafting out of the kitchen. Nothing beats the smell of frying bacon. You gotta love bacon. I think I'm hungry. I'm going to go eat. Bye.

October 27

Dear Me,

Okay, where was I? Ah, yes. My first encounter with Ruth. *Godulous* for sure! In normal circumstances, I would have been spending that day in jail or in the psychiatric ward of the local hospital. Instead, I was eating homemade bread, scrambled eggs, and crisp bacon, served on ivory china with a silver rim that was elegant yet simple, a lot like my hostess. She kept asking me questions and feeding me. I kept eating to avoid answering all the questions.

"Well, Vanessa. You still haven't told me what was going on last night?"

"No. It's just ..."

"It's okay. You can tell me. It is obvious that you need some help, beyond what I've given you here, and I believe I can give you that help if I knew what you needed. Does that make sense?"

"Yes. It's just, I'm so ... ashamed."

"No need, Vanessa. We've all gotten ourselves in pickles before. Fortunately, we have a God who can pick us up and dust us off."

Oh great, another religious one, I thought to myself. *What was it with me and religious people?* I wanted nothing to do with it. I had had it with spiritual stuff. I was sticking with suicide therapy—much quicker and clearer in my opinion. Nevertheless, the last thing I wanted to do was shock this nice church lady with my disgusting self. So, I reverted to my childhood habit of making up some story to make myself look better than I really was. I thought I'd make myself look like a victim instead of an idiot. Here she was trying to help and love me, and I looked her straight in her saggy-skinned eyes and made up some cockamamie story (how do you spell ca-ca-mame-ee, anyway?). I made up some outlandish story to make her feel sorry for me instead of repulsed.

"My fiancé died."

"Oh, my dear girl. I'm so sorry."

Sniffle, sniffle.

"What happened?"

"He was murdered. A drive-by shooting."

"Good heavens, this world we live in! When did this happen, dear?"

"A couple of months ago."

"Where?"

"L.A. We had gone to a U2 concert. He proposed to me there in the Hollywood Bowl. We had had such a nice time. Then he got shot."

"Dear Lord. Were you with him?"

"Yes, the bullet went through his head and right through the window on my side. I had bent over to pick out a tape to play." Pretty good stuff, huh? I should be a writer.

"Praise God! His angels were with you."

"I wish they hadn't bothered." I had finally told some shred of truth, which made the tears start flowing for real.

"Hush, now. Hush. You poor baby. I know it seems like the easiest way, just to end it, but God has other plans for you. It's not your time."

"I want it to be," I cried.

"No. No you don't. Why did you stop?"

She had a point. "I don't know. It was the sign."

"What sign?"

"In front of the church. About not leaving earth without Jesus. I don't know why. It just made me stop."

"Well, you see? Jesus is calling out to you. That's why you stopped. He wanted us to meet."

"Yeah, right."

"Yes, right. You're here for a reason. Don't leave without finding out what it is."

"I've got to go." I didn't know where to, but I had a panicky feeling welling up in my throat that if I didn't leave, I'd have a heart attack or something. I stood up and grabbed my bag.

"Thank you for everything. You've been so nice. Thank you." I dragged my bag out the door and stumbled halfway down the stairs. I landed at the bottom, on my bottom, and cried uncontrollably. Once again, I'm surprised nobody called the police.

I don't know why I didn't put myself out of my misery that night. Well, I do know, but it still surprises the more practical side of me. Ruth was right. Jesus was calling me. He had a plan. And regardless of how desperately stupid and self-centered I had become, He was giving me another chance to try it His way. I was not willing. Yet. But despite my fatalistic thought life, I wasn't ready to try my way yet either.

I wandered around the San Francisco streets, talking to myself. I was starring in my own ridiculous cartoon show, with a little angel popping up on one shoulder and a little devil popping up on the other.

"Go ahead, just get it over with, you worthless baby-killing dependent lesbian with nowhere to go and no one to turn to."

"Go back to Ruth's. She'll take you in. You can get through this."

"No, you can't survive. All you ever do is make a mess out of things. You even gave your own father cancer with your deranged thoughts. Just end it. It's over anyway."

Back and forth I went, wishing someone would hit me over the head with an Acme frying pan to end the show. Godulously, I somehow ended up back at the bottom of Ruth's stairs.

She didn't even seem surprised to see me. Ratty hair and all.

"I've made some cranberry-orange bread this morning. Want some?"

October 28

Dear Me,

From the day Ruth found me at her door, I was in a fight for my life.

The first mistake I made was not to recant my lies. I was too prideful, I guess. I was still so confused at that point, that when she mentioned my tragedy and the effects of unresolved grief on a person's life, I didn't even realize she wasn't referring to my actual circumstances. I just let things be. Of course that came back to bite me later, as all lies eventually do, but I'll get to that later.

"Do you have a place to stay?" asked Ruth with a mouth full of cranberry-orange bread.

"No."

"What about your family? Where are they?"

"Up north. Arcata."

"Ah, yes. Do they know where you are?"

"No."

"Don't you think you should tell them?"

"I don't know where I am. I figured I'd wait until I got things figured out."

"You can tell them you're staying with me if you'd like."

I looked around the room at the quiet yet richly decorated room, with antiques and watercolor paintings all over the place. "I can't afford to live here. I don't even have a job."

"Nonsense. I need a companion. My son has been pestering me to place an ad in the classifieds. I told him that you never know what kind of weirdo you end up with from the newspaper. I knew that the right one would come along, and here you are."

"You're too nice. But I'm quite certain that I'm exactly what you had in mind when you used the term 'weirdo.' I can't stay here."

"Yes, you can. You have a lovely face and a need. I have a lovely heart and a need. It works perfectly. I don't need your money. I need your time, your friendship, and a little help with housecleaning. You need a safe place to stay. Problems solved."

"Are you sure?" Not like I had a lot of options.

"Of course I am. I've got a job for you too. Isn't it wonderful how the Lord works?"

She was beside herself with excitement. I was confused. But she made good bread. And her home was beautiful.

It was not like any other "grandma home" I'd ever been in. I don't mean to be rude, but in my experience everyone over sixty-five seemed to order their decorations from the same catalog. But no split-seamed couches covered by polyester or plastic could be found. No smell of artificial roses, poodle pee, arthritis ointment, or lemon tea. It smelled of fresh flowers from the overflowing vases in every room. The furniture was antique and well-maintained, even though she actually allowed people to sit on it. Each of the bedrooms was decorated in coordinated themes, and none of them smelled musty, despite lack of use. She let me pick which of the three unused rooms I wanted.

The first one she showed me was exquisite. It had a queen-sized brass bed, walnut wardrobe, and a sitting area in the corner. The bed was draped in what looked like an antique Queen Anne's lace cover. The carpet was a plush rose-colored pile with a small floral area rug at the foot of the bed. On the walls hung paintings of lush flower gardens in walnut frames. The overall effect reminded me of a room that would be in one of those fancy Mendocino bed and breakfast inns. Great to visit, but not home.

The second room was much smaller. The far wall held a day bed covered with an obviously homemade quilt and a dozen or so throw pillows. A small oak armoire and matching dressing table completed the furniture. The walls were painted a pale yellow and the only picture was an enlarged black-and-white photograph of the ocean with the sun nearly set in the distance. I walked closer to the picture to get a better look. At the bottom of the picture, almost hidden, was a woman in a flowing white dress, with her back to the camera. She was playing the violin.

"Is that you?" I asked.

"No. I don't know who it is. Paul, my husband, always carried his camera around, just in case he saw something worth capturing on film. We were taking a Sunday drive one evening when we saw the remarkable sunset. He stopped and took the picture from the side of the road. It wasn't until we got it developed that we even noticed the woman."

"That's amazing. It's beautiful."

"Yes, I know. It is very special to me."

She didn't have to show me the other room. "I'll take this one."

"I thought you might," she said, smiling. "Why don't you get cleaned up and then come down to talk about where we go from here. Deal?"

"Okay." I couldn't stop staring at the picture.

"Ever been a hostess before?" Ruth asked when I came downstairs smelling a good bit better.

"Excuse me?"

"In a restaurant? Ever been a hostess before?"

"No."

"Oh, well, it's not hard. We've been looking for a hostess for the restaurant and we're getting desperate. Opening night is tomorrow."

"Whoa. Back up a minute. Who's 'we' and what restaurant?"

"'We' is my son, Dale, and yours truly. He's the chef and I'm the waitress et al. The restaurant is Solomon's. It's right up the road and is going to be a huge success. And we need a great hostess to give all of our customers a warm smile and pleasant start to their dining experience. Interested?"

"I guess so. But what if your son doesn't want to hire some crazy lady you found swimming in a pool of vodka?"

"I've already told him about you. He trusts me. You've got the job if you want it. Like I said, we're desperate."

"Well in that case ..."

"Great. We need to get you some clothes. Are you hungry?"

"No."

"Good. I'm sure Dale wants us to try his opening night special for lunch. Hope you don't mind being a culinary guinea pig. It's in your job description."

"No, I guess not."

"Don't worry. I've never had anything too awful, and I've been doing it for years. Except for that calamari stew with mushrooms and eggplant. Keep the squid in the sea, not on my dinner plate, please."

"Who's Solomon?"

"Ahh. A long story that I can tell you while we walk to Macy's to get you some clothing."

"I don't have any money."

"I know. It's a business expense."

Things were moving so fast. Move fast or die.

Walking to Union Square, I learned some Jacobson family history. Ruth had lived in San Francisco for thirty years with her husband of forty years. He had always wanted to open up his own restaurant, but when Dale showed an interest in the culinary arts, he put his money toward training Dale at the best schools and saving for the time when maybe they could go into business together. Dale went to the Culinary Institute of America for a while, but he didn't like New York. He came home and finished training at the California Culinary Academy.

"Unfortunately, a month after they started seriously looking into buying a place, Paul had his first heart attack," Ruth explained. "His doctor told him to slow down and lay off the high-fat food. Which is like telling a professional boxer to stop letting people hit him so much. Not going to happen. And it didn't. He had another heart attack just after Christmas last year. That one he didn't survive"

"I'm so sorry."

"Dale has had an especially hard time. He feels guilty that he kept his dad from fulfilling his dream. But you can't question why these things happen. You just trust the Lord. He knows what He's doing better than we do. I miss Paul, but I know we'll be together again."

I ignored her religious outburst, excusing it as a symptom of old age. "So I guess Dale is really anxious to make this place work?"

"Yes. We used his dad's money to buy it. We were both a little surprised at the cost. But it's worked out so perfectly, and we both know it is what his dad would have wanted. It's like King David in the Bible. He wanted to build a temple to the Lord but God said sorry, it's a great idea, but you won't be the one ... it will be your son, Solomon. So, we named it Solomon's. Bound for success."

Like Ebola, but with much more pleasant results, I caught Ruth's optimism. It at least took my mind off everything else.

October 29

Dear Me,

"What did you think of me when you first met me?" Dale asked with his cute grin. I felt like such a heel having to tell him the truth. No sparks. No flutters in the tummy. No sting of cupid's arrow. Nothing. All I could think when I first met Dale Jacobson was that Ruth could never disown him. They were clones.

"That you were your mother minus the gray perm."

"Now that's romantic," he pouted.

Truth hurts. There was nothing romantic about my first encounter with Dale.

"Vanessa, I've been so excited to meet you."

"Hi." Enthusiasm obviously ran in the family.

"I can't tell you what an answer to prayer you are. Not only as a companion for Mom here, but as our hostess too. Are you sure you know what you're getting into?" He laughed Ruth's laugh.

"I just hope you all won't be sorry," I said.

"Oh, we won't. I know it. Like I said, you're our answer to prayer."

Perfect. Two fanatics.

"I'll do my best."

"Well, let's get you guys fed. Did you get your shopping done?"

"Yes, sir. She's ready to go," said Ruth.

"Want some lunch?"

"Sure."

"I'm trying out a saffron risotto shrimp dish for tomorrow's special. You'll have to tell me what you think."

"Oh, I'm no culinary expert. When I'm hungry, a Whopper tastes pretty good to me."

"Oh my, it's worse than I thought. Mother, thank God you rescued this poor girl. She needs some deprogramming, and fast."

"Well, if anyone can do it, it's you, dear."

"Sit, my friend. You are about to be cured of that nasty Whopper craving forever." He disappeared behind the two-way swinging doors.

He was right. I haven't had a Whopper since. Ruth was right too. Solomon's was a great success. Opening night was full of jitters and running around. Since it was just starting out, we had very little staff. Dale was the chef, Manuel the veggie chopper/dish washer/occasional busboy, Ruth the waitress/occasional busboy, and me—hostess/occasional waitress and busboy or whatever else needed to be done. My specialty.

Just before the doors were to open at 5:00 PM, Dale called us all together and prayed for the night. I stood there with my eyes wide open, wondering how on earth I had gotten there. But as always, the Jacobsons' optimistic enthusiasm took over, and I let myself relax in the world of these really weirdly wonderful people.

Dale had a friend at the *Chronicle* with some clout, so they had a preopening plug in the entertainment section. An up-and-coming vocalist who was performing in an off-Broadway hit—another friend of a friend—performed in the lobby. The place wasn't packed, but the flow was constant and the crowd full of compliments.

I liked the professional feel of the straight black skirt and loose silk blouse Ruth and I had picked out at Macy's. I had never dressed up for work before. It felt like a real job.

Ruth, in her classy pantsuit, worked with the energy of three teenagers. She remained calm and unflustered and made everyone feel at home. I had to help her serve a couple tables during a few rushes, but she handled herself with charm, and I tried to follow her lead. It was obvious that if things continued on so well, Dale would have to hire at least one more server. Dale was ecstatic when the last customer left at 1:00 AM.

"Can you believe it? What a night."

"Of course I believe it. We said it was going to fly, didn't we?" Ruth said.

"I know. But man ... it was better than I imagined. I'm totally beat, but I don't think I could sleep a wink. I'm too excited."

"Well, have a seat, Chefy Boy. I'll get you a cup of decaf and a bowl of soup. I bet you haven't eaten a thing, have you?"

"No, Ma'am, I haven't," he said in mock submission. "Make it a soda instead; I'm too hot for coffee. Come sit with me, Vanessa."

I sat.

"How do you feel?"

"Tired and my feet are killing me," I said taking off my black flats, thankful I had taken Ruth's advice against the high-heeled boots. "It was a great night." Foot in hand.

"Wasn't it? And you did perfectly. What'd I tell you?"

"Well, I felt good about it. When we start getting more reservations and stuff, I'm sure it will get harder. But Ruth was amazing."

"She is great, isn't she?" he asked, knowing that she was right behind him with his soda. "Ahh, speak of the devil ..."

"Not in front of me you don't. I prefer to speak of more pleasant things."

So there I sat. Night after night, morning after morning, with a family that was not my own. I shared little bits of myself. The tiniest of bits. Afraid of giving too much and having to keep up the front of my lies. I did my job. I enjoyed myself. But I went to bed with the same fears, the same dreams, the same baggie of pills hidden in my underwear drawer.

I suppose it would have gone on like that if it wasn't for another one of those too-weird-to-be-a-coincidence things that happened about three months later.

November 1

Dear Me,

One of the quirky-fun things about Solomon's that made it such a success was its catering to the up-and-coming music talent of the Bay Area. Every weekend, we would feature a local talent who was struggling to break into the limelight. Head shots pasted on poster board were placed on an outside easel, advertising that weekend's performer. Dale's newspaper friend often featured our guests in his column. A few had found regular jobs after appearing at Solomon's. Usually it was a singer. Sometimes it was an instrumentalist. Usually it was a great success. Sometimes it was a huge flop.

Like the time Danny, our newly hired waiter, begged Dale to let his cousin fill in for a last-minute Saturday cancellation.

"What does he do?" Dale asked.

"Oh, sing and stuff. He's really talented," said Danny.

"Okay, call him."

That particular Saturday was more packed than usual. We were running on full speed when the most horrendous sound brought us to a screeching halt. It was like a movie. Forks stopped halfway from plate to mouth, glasses stopped clinking, people stopped chewing, when

"Johnny Blue Jeans," as his poster read, started tuning his one-man-band machine. It was a complete sideshow get-up with harmonica, accordion, cymbals, bass drum, and horn, in whose bell he had placed the microphone prior to tuning.

He played on and on like a wind-up monkey, only pausing to tell a really bad joke in between sets, and I started to think that he was drunk as well as severely out of his element. Several patrons complained. Two couples left. And the fiasco led to a none-too-flattering write-up in the Sunday paper. Danny was devastated.

"I'm so sorry, Dale. I had no idea he was going to do that. He used to sing and play the piano when we were kids. He was really good. I don't know what he was thinking."

"I think he was several shots past thinking," Dale said, laughing.

"Oh man, boss. I'm so sorry. I just don't know what to say."

"It's not your fault, Danny. I agreed to have him come. You didn't know. It's over. Don't worry about it."

"Yeah, but the paper. What a mess."

"Oh, who cares about the paper. If I believed people came here just for the entertainment, I'd be throwing in the towel right now. I think they like my food, and I didn't blow that, I don't think."

Danny finally started to laugh.

"Come on. Water under the bridge. Anyway, I've got this dynamo pianist coming next Saturday. From what I hear about him, no one will be able to remember what happened last night. I'm not mad, okay? Why don't you go write the special on the board?"

"Sure, boss. What is it?"

"'Johnny-Blue-Jeans' Liver and Brussels Sprouts—it will be a huge hit." He laughed his way into the kitchen.

You've probably guessed it. *He* was the dynamite pianist.

You can imagine my reaction when Kenneth's perfect, smiling face greeted me from the easel placed beside the front door. I thought I was going to throw up.

Wise is the old adage, "Never lie, because sooner or later your lie grows legs and comes back to kick you in the rear." Okay, so it might not be an official adage (what is an adage?), but it is wise nonetheless. My carefully built web of lies began to unravel. Needless to say, I did not handle this event very well.

"Here she is. Vanessa, come here. I want you to meet someone," yelled Dale from the side lounge. "Vanessa Palmer, this is Kenneth Broderick, the pianist I told you about."

I didn't—couldn't—say anything.

"Hi, Vanessa. Fancy meeting you here," Kenneth said, smiling a condescending smile I'm sure I once thought was charming. He reached for my hand.

"You know each other?" Dale was surprised.

"Yes, we went to school together a few years ago. Matter of fact, we lived together a few years ago."

I wanted to run.

"Really?"

"You better watch this one. One day she's there, the next she's gone and you don't hear from her again."

I stood there and stared at him dumbly with my stomach in my throat. I tried to talk, to laugh, to act casually. But I just kept getting hotter. My palms and pits were sweating. I thought I was going to lose my pecan bread with honey on the baby grand piano. I panicked. I ran out the door.

It had never occurred to me that I might see him again. I thought for sure that he'd be in New York or Paris, living out our dreams with the beautiful blonde. I had trained myself not to think about him. I never let my mind linger on the vague images of our life together that had been blurred by drinking and meditating on "happy thoughts." I didn't want to give them the chance to come into focus. I didn't want to see with the eyes of my heart the love I had for him. Seeing him every night in my dreams was enough.

Seeing him for real was like being a contestant on some sadist game show, "This Is Your Nightmare," where they reenact your deepest, darkest, sweat-producing dream to see if you can survive. I couldn't. I lost miserably.

I spent the night wondering where I would go to consume my pills this time. I guess I was polite enough not to consider killing myself in Ruth's house. She was so nice, after all, and I figured that would put a damper on even her perpetually happy disposition.

I went downstairs early to get a drink of water. I hadn't slept much, if at all. I must have looked pretty bad.

"Oh, what on earth are you doing out of bed?" Ruth asked from her chair in the corner where she spent her mornings drinking coffee, reading her Bible, and praying for miserable souls like mine.

"I just came to get some water. I didn't mean to interrupt you."

"Nonsense. I just wish you had called me to get it. You're sick and need to rest."

"I'm not sick, Ruth. I just haven't slept much."

"Well, Dale said you weren't feeling well and that's why you came home."

"Dale was being nice. I came home because I panicked when I saw someone I used to know. I'm sorry I let you guys down."

"You didn't let us down. We were busy, yes, but we managed. You didn't have to run."

"Yes. I think I did."

"Kenneth was such a nice man. Such a talent."

"Yes. I know."

"Do you want to talk about him?"

"No. I don't really know what to say."

"Sit. I'll get you coffee."

"No. I'll get it. You don't need to wait on me."

"I know, but I do need to move this old bag of bones around before it gets stuck in this chair. Sit. I'll be right back."

My head was pounding. What was I going to say to this nice woman? If only she knew who I really was.

"So, you lived with him, huh?" she said as she backed through the swinging door that separated the kitchen from the living room.

"Yes. For a while."

"Was this before or after your fiancé died?"

"Before," I said to my lap. If I had looked her in the eye, I would have seen that she had me figured out already. That she knew I'd been lying to her. But I stared at my coffee cup and tried to keep up with my web of lies.

"He said you were studying music. The cello was it?"

"Yeah."

"I thought you were taking courses in business. That's quite a ways from the performing arts, isn't it?"

"I couldn't make it as a musician."

"That's not what Kenneth said. He was flabbergasted when he learned we didn't even know you played the cello. He said you were the best he'd ever heard."

"He did?" I looked at her.

"Yes. He asked where you were playing, and we said nowhere that we knew of. Do you play anymore, Vanessa?"

"No. Not for years."

"Why not? If you are as good as he says, and I know he must be a good judge of talent, it seems such a waste—"

I started to cry. "Stop. I don't want to talk about it. I can't play anymore. I'm sorry I couldn't handle seeing him last night. I'm an idiot. I'll work until you find someone new. I'm so sorry to have let you all down."

"Whoa! Slow down, girl. Why on God's green earth would we need to replace you, Vanessa? Because you missed a night of work?"

"I left you hanging."

"You were shaken. Things obviously ended badly between you two. I'm sure you were quite shocked to see him last night."

I nodded.

"I understand that."

"I doubt it."

"I don't understand what you were feeling, but the feelings were real nonetheless. Why don't you give me a try? I'm not so naïve as you think. I've been around the block a few times."

Yeah, right.

"You think I've always been like I am today? That I have no skeletons in my closet?"

"I'm sure my skeletons are much larger."

"Perhaps. But I have a few. Let's see ... what's a good one? Do you know where I met Dale's father? At my fiancé's birthday party. They were second cousins."

"Really?" So I was a little surprised.

"Yep. I'm not proud of it, but for two months I saw both of them. Right up to the week before my wedding. Finally I came to my senses and called off the wedding. But not before I broke a good man's heart and wasted much of my parents' hard-earned money."

"Well ..."

"I'm not trying to one-up you on past indiscretions. I don't want to pry into something you don't want to share. But that being said, know that you can talk to me about it if you want. Or not. Whatever you wish. What you can't do is think that something from your past negates your obligation to the restaurant. We aren't going to let you go that easily."

"But—"

"No buts. You will come back and bring that charm of yours with you. We need you."

"Yeah, right."

She grabbed my arm. "We need you, Vanessa."

I fell to my knees at the foot of her chair and laid my head in her lap. She stroked my hair, and I cried for what seemed like hours. When I finally looked up at her through my swollen, burning eyes, she smiled down at me and said, "Next week, we've booked a thirteen-year-old opera aria whistler touring from Florida. You don't know him, do you?"

We laughed.

November 2

Dear Me,

There's a passage in the Bible that drives me crazy. It's somewhere in the gospels when Jesus is talking to His disciples about "love thine enemies." It says something to the effect that if someone strikes you on the face, turn so he can get the other side, and if someone steals your jacket, give him your pants too.

I'm starting to understand it better now. If Dale had treated me like I deserved after that incident—if he had fired me, shunned me, reprimanded me, anything—I would have continued in my self-pitying, "I'm-a-pathetic-loser" frame of mind. Instead, he fixed me a special lunch. He asked my advice on future entertainment ideas. He told me that he'd love to hear me play my cello someday. And when I said I didn't play anymore, he dropped the subject. He accepted my apology when I told him I was sorry. He asked if I wanted to talk about it and accepted that I didn't. He made me feel at ease, when I thought I'd feel like a fool forever. And because of it, I accepted his invitation to go out to brunch with him on the coming Sunday—after church. If that's not proof of the power of kindness, nothing is. I agreed to go to church. With a man.

"We were just talking about you," Ruth said from her favorite perch when I came down for breakfast that Sunday.

A few weeks back, I would have looked around the room for guests, but I knew by then what she meant. She was talking to God. Praying. Not in the way I'd always thought of praying—hands folded, eyes closed, kneeling on the floor if needed. No. Ruth talked to God like she talked to anyone, matter-of-factly and constantly. And though I was starting to get used to her holy ways, I still was pretty uncomfortable knowing that she was talking to Him about me. "What about?" I asked, not really sure I wanted to know.

"Oh, this and that. Mostly that you'd be open to hear from Him at church today."

"Hear from Him? You mean like He'll make a special appearance just for me?"

"Of course. You won't see Him, but He'll be there, calling you to Him."

"I wouldn't be so sure. I haven't thought too highly of Him over the years."

"Ah, nonetheless, He's waiting for you."

I dropped it. Ruth wasn't pushy or obnoxious in her beliefs. She believed what she believed and wasn't afraid to show it. But her confidence was still unnerving. I didn't want to know what her expectations were because I was sure I would not meet them. "Any coffee left?"

"Of course. You'd better eat a little something before you go. I hate it when my stomach growls in the middle of the sermon."

"Do you need anything?"

"No. I'm done. Help yourself."

"Are you sure?"

"Yes, dear. I'm going to go get ready. The older I get, the longer it takes to put on my Sunday best."

I poked my head out of the kitchen. "I don't have any 'best.' Is my black skirt and a sweater okay?"

"Of course, dear. Do you think God has a dress code? He doesn't care. I'm just an old dog who can't learn any new tricks. You can wear blue jeans if you want."

"I'll stick with the skirt." I went back in the kitchen for toast.

"Vanessa?"

"Yeah?"

"I'm really glad you're coming."

"Thank you. Me too." I was really more interested in the brunch afterward. Dale had been occupying a bit more of my thoughts each day.

Dale picked us up in his Volvo station wagon at nine. It was a bright sunny day with deceptively cold temperatures. It was the first week of December, and it was beginning to look a lot like Christmas all around town. I figured I'd freeze when I saw the hard mahogany pews in the gray stone church building. But the atmosphere was warm. The sun was shining through the stained glass above the pulpit, along with the twinkling Christmas lights from the huge tree, and sent splashes of cheery color around the room. It felt good.

"How do you think Joseph felt?" the minister asked the congregation. "He was engaged. He'd been waiting like a good boy, keeping a proper distance from his betrothed. You think Joseph's urges weren't the same as ours just because he lived a long time ago? You think testosterone wasn't raging in the young men of biblical times? Joseph had been riding his donkey home after every Friday night date with beautiful Mary and dousing his head with cold water from the well. He was a good man. But he was a man."

I'd certainly never heard talk like this in a church before.

"How do you think he felt when Mary came over

and said, 'Honey, we need to talk'? What would you have done if your fiancée said, 'I know we've been waiting until we get married and all, but some guy appeared to me today and told me that I am pregnant. Don't be mad. Oh, and by the way, he said that the baby was the Lord, the Messiah, and we're to name him Jesus'?

"'Jesus? I promised Ma we'd name the first born Joe Jr.'

"How do you think he felt? Joseph had every right to throw her out. He had every right to tell her that she was crazy. He had every right to have her stoned to death, for that was the appropriate punishment for adultery during those times. He had every right to pout and cry and be mad at God. 'Why me, Lord? What have I done to deserve this humiliation? This shame? I did all the right things.' Didn't he? Didn't he have the right?"

Everyone was nodding in unison.

"Of course he did. But he didn't do any of those things. Not one. Instead, he protected her. He ignored the stares and comments of the townspeople. He took her to Bethlehem and did all he could to provide for her when the baby was born. He agreed to more trips to the cold well and waited even longer to consummate his marriage, until after the baby was born. He took on the role of father to a boy he did not conceive, a boy who would never really be his, and he loved Him as any father loves his son.

"Joseph was a good man. He was God's chosen earthly father of His son. Quite a job. But he was just a man. He had no super powers, no divine specifications.

He was just an ordinary man asked to do something extraordinary.

"I ask all of you today: What would you have done? What do you do when your life takes a path you never expected? How do you respond to the disappointments? The challenges? The temptations? Do you cower away? Do you feel sorry for yourself and pout? Do you get angry at the perpetrator? At God? Do you refuse to forgive and accept God's will for your life? Do you continue on your own path and ignore God completely?"

Did he really want me to answer those questions?

"Life's rough. Sometimes it downright stinks, doesn't it? But don't you think our God is big enough to make something good out of the messes we make? Don't you think God is wise enough to know how it's all going to work out in the end, even when we cannot or will not see?

"What if God had chosen you instead of Joseph? What would you have done? What will you do next time life throws you a curve ball? Do you have the courage to be Joseph? To say, 'Okay God, I don't get it, but I'll do it anyway.' I challenge you today—be a Joseph. You never know what God has in store for you."

We sang a few more hymns and filed out the back of the church, shaking the pastor's hand as we went out the door.

"That was some sermon, wasn't it?" Dale said as we got in the car.

"It sure was. I just love how Pastor Harvey makes you think. He doesn't just hand us everything on a golden platter. We have to work a little," said Ruth.

"What did you think, Vanessa?" he asked.

"It was good. Different from what I've heard before, that's for sure."

"How so?"

"It was so, I don't know, real. Not mystical or spiritual at all, really. I've always thought religion was supposed to be mystical—otherworldly, you know?"

"I suppose many religions are that way. But our faith, true Christian faith, is not a religion," he responded.

"What's that supposed to mean?" I asked.

"It's a relationship. It's not about the prayers we say or the words we recite. It's not about doing all the right things or honoring certain saints. It is about choosing to have a relationship with Jesus Christ. It's completely different from any other religion."

"Hmmm." I had no idea what he was talking about.

"You don't mind if we drop you off here, do you, Mom?" Dale asked, pulling up to the curb in front of her house.

"Of course not. I told you I could have walked home."

"It's too cold for that. Be careful going up the steps."

"Oh stop your mothering, Son. I am fine. You two have a good time. Eat a hot roll with some of that homemade honey butter for me, okay?"

"You bet."

After Ruth got out of the car, I started to get nervous. This was starting to feel more like a date, and I hadn't been on one of those in a very long time.

We drove to a little café on the pier that overlooked the water. We sat at a small table and I devoured four of the rolls with homemade honey butter. I was hungry and nervous.

"So, what did you really think of church today?" he asked again after our Eggs Benedict came.

"It was nice, really. I've never heard a preacher talk like he did."

"Where have you gone to church before?"

"Nowhere really. My family never went much. What about you?" Anything to get the focus off of me and my religious background.

"Well, I had the advantage of being raised with parents who believed in God. They always were reading the Bible and bringing us to church to learn about Jesus. Mom, especially, has always been passionate about Jesus and the Bible. I don't remember a time when she wasn't talking about it."

"There's no doubt that she believes it wholeheartedly," I said.

"Yeah. I started to think she was pretty weird when I got to be about thirteen. Everything your parents do is weird at that age. I stopped buying into all the God stuff she was always spouting. I decided to do my own thing, be the prodigal son, you know."

"No, not really. I only went to church on holidays or for funerals, remember. I'm a little foggy about all the Bible stories you guys are always talking about."

"Sorry, don't mean to get 'churchy' on you. There's a story in the Bible about a boy who demanded his inheritance from his father early, and then went off and squandered it all on women and drinking and general debauchery. Soon, he found himself living in a pigsty, wishing for the food the pigs were eating and pining for home. He finally crawled back home, planning to beg for a job as a hired hand for his father, for he knew he was completely unworthy of being his son. But when his father saw him coming, he ran to him, gave him a cloak of honor and a ring of gold and ordered his servants to kill the fatted calf for a feast. His son had returned."

"So, you went off drinking and womanizing at thirteen?" I laughed.

"Well, not exactly. But I did start flirting with rebellion. I would skip school and smoke cigarettes behind the backstop at school. Seemingly harmless kid stuff, but it just led to more and more, and eventually ... well, I got myself busted."

"Busted? What did you do?" I had a hard time believing this straight-laced guy had ever even lied before.

"Toward the end of my junior year, I vandalized the high school with a bunch of my buddies. We spray-painted, broke windows, and trashed classrooms. Really brilliant stuff. The cops came and threw us in jail. The rest of them got bailed out that night. Mom and Dad let me stay there the night."

"You're kidding me!"

"No. They wanted me to suffer the consequences of what I had done. They wanted me to realize that there wasn't an easy way out of the wrong decisions I'd made."

"Were you mad?"

"At first, because I was so scared. There weren't exactly the friendliest people hanging out in the jail that night. This young white boy was a great target for harassment."

"Yeah, I know what you mean," I said.

"You do? When have you ever spent a night in jail?" he laughed incredulously.

"Oh, it's a long story. I'll tell you about it some time."

"Okay." He was momentarily baffled but easily dissuaded.

"So what happened?" I asked.

"The next morning, my mom and dad came to get me. They hugged me and told me they loved me. Then they asked what I planned to do about this mess I had made. I knew that even though I had embarrassed them and broken the law, they still loved me as much as ever. They showed me unconditional love. And I understood for the first time, in that stinking jail cell, the depth of God's love for me. He saw me for what I was, a fallen, stupid, selfish kid, and He loved me anyway, He died on the cross to pay for my sins, and wanted to live in my imperfect heart, so that I could live with Him in heaven one day. I hugged my parents, worked my tail off in community service and mowing lawns to pay my fines, and turned my life over to Christ once and for all."

"So you just turned around and never looked back?"

"For the most part. I'm not perfect, that's for sure, but I keep on walking with Jesus."

"Hmmm. Good eggs, huh?" My subtle way of changing the subject.

"Glad you like them." He allowed the diversion, and

we had a very pleasant day together. But I couldn't stop thinking about everything I had heard.

Then the phone rang.

November 4

Dear Me,

I don't know if I'll ever get over my irrational fear of unexpected phone calls. To this day, if the phone rings late at night or early in the morning, my mind instantly races to all the dark places and tragic possibilities. Panic attack. Then it ends up being a wrong number or some discourteous telemarketing call and it takes me a half an hour to recover. Anyway, I was happy, enjoying life, flirting a bit with my boss, and having the best birthday celebration ever.

Did I mention it was my birthday? Ruth took me out to celebrate and got me a complete makeover that was so much fun. I hadn't even thought about my pill bag in at least two days. Then the phone rang. Perhaps I should back up.

Rewind.

Okay. It was my birthday.

During a silly game we (me, Dale, Ruth, and Danny)

played after closing the night before, where someone was supposed to be able to guess your weight by calculating your height, shoe size, and birthday numbers (don't ask, it didn't work very well), Ruth discovered the next day was my birthday.

"That's tomorrow. Your birthday is *tomorrow?*" squealed Ruth in a high-pitched voice reserved for her incredulous moments.

"Yeah, I guess it is," I said as though I had just realized it.

"Why didn't you tell me?"

"I just didn't think of it. It's not a big deal."

"Yes it is. Tell her Dale. Is it a big deal?"

"Yep. Big deal, sure is a big deal," he said with a grin.

"I've got plans to make. Appointments to schedule. How am I supposed to do all that with no warning?"

"You don't have to do anything, Ruth. Really."

"Oh yes I do. Don't I, Dale? Tell her that I have to do something."

"Yep, she's got to make her plans." Now he was laughing.

"You guys are making me nervous," I said. My face was hot. I really hated them making a big deal about it, but I loved it at the same time.

"Dale, you make lunch reservations for the two of you and plan for Danny and Mike to take over the lunch crowd. I'll call Monica at home to see if she can squeeze you in tomorrow morning."

"Squeeze me in where?" Now I was really nervous.

"At Gina's Day Spa. It's a Jacobson tradition. The

women of the family have to be pampered on their birthday. It's makeover time, darling."

"But I can't. I'm—"

"You'd better take me home; we have an early morning."

"Yep. You'd better go." Dale patted my back.

"I don't have much choice, do I?"

"Not a bit. Let's go."

Ruth was true to her word. She brought me breakfast in bed. Dale brought me yellow roses. We were at Gina's by nine.

I had not put much effort into my appearance since leaving UOP. At first, I was too drunk to care what I looked like. Alice believed any emphasis on outward beauty was useless and fleeting. If one's inner self was healthy and pampered, then the outer self would naturally glow. When I took a good long look at myself in the mirror, I realized that my inner self was obviously in pretty bad shape. I did not glow. I looked washed out, tired, pale, and old.

I was embarrassed at how bad I looked when Monica turned me around in the swivel chair and asked, "So, what should we do with this?"

My once long, curly, shining hair, after being chopped off above my ears and then left to grow out with no shaping at all, was frizzy and dull. I was in the habit of twisting it and clamping it above my neck with a cheap jaw clip. "Whatever it takes."

"That's the spirit, Vanessa," said Ruth from the seat next to me. "Let's show 'em what you've got."

Four hours and I'm sure several hundred dollars later, I was a new woman, revamped and pampered from head to toe.

"Well, God made the world in six days, but Monica made a new woman in a few short hours," Ruth squealed with delight when she saw me.

I had to admit, I looked good. My hair was cut in a jaw-length bob, natural curl framed my face, deep conditioning and a few golden highlights made it shine. Facial, manicure, pedicure, and massage—heck, I was beautiful.

"Oh, Ruth. Thank you. Thank you so much. This is the best birthday present I've ever had."

"It wasn't me. Thank Monica."

"I did. But I never would have known how much I needed this. I feel so good."

"You look terrific. Let's go get you a new dress, something to go with that glamorous new 'do."

I was flying high and feeling good about myself as we walked back to Solomon's. Dale's response was better than the present. He was utterly speechless. He took me to lunch. We held hands. I felt like a real person. I felt alive and like I might just stay that way for awhile. We got back to the restaurant in time for the dinner crowd to start, and Ruth met us at the door. She was holding a Post-it note.

"Your mother called."

"My mother?"

"Yes, dear. Mine has been dead for years."

"What did she want?"

"To wish you a happy birthday, I'm sure, and to tell you that they are in town."

"In town. Here?"

"Yes, dear. Here."

"Why?"

"I don't know. You'll have to ask them tonight."

"Tonight?"

"Yes, dear. So many questions. They are coming here, in an hour. I thought we'd have a special celebration. That's okay, isn't it?"

"Yes, of course. I'm just surprised. I haven't seen them in awhile." I was lying—it was far from okay.

I had worked very hard at not thinking about my parents. It was not fair, I know that, but I blamed pretty much all of my problems on them. I had made a load of mistakes and had many lapses in moral judgment since I'd left home. I did a wonderful job of screwing up my life all by myself. Nevertheless, I needed a scapegoat in order to survive. They were the easiest targets. No, it did not matter that my dad had cancer. No, it did not matter that I believed I was ultimately the cause of that cancer. They had never accepted me, which set up a pattern of seeking acceptance from others, despite the cost to me. *They* were to blame. How's that for self-psycho analysis?

Now, despite all my efforts to keep them out of my life, they were coming into my New World. I didn't want them there. But I was stuck, because if I explained to Ruth and Dale how much I didn't want them to come, then they would realize how truly screwed up I was. They'd see through the illusion of normalcy I had been painting for them. The lies would be exposed. The gig would be up. I was going to have to put on a good front and act like the loving daughter I wasn't.

Before I could properly process all of these thoughts and pull myself together, they were there, standing in the waiting area. Waiting.

Dying.

Dad was thin, sunken, bald, and stooped. He dragged an oxygen tank behind him on a cart attached to a tube attached to his nose. The three-foot walk from the curbside, where the cab had dropped them off, into the restaurant had tired him. He coughed and wheezed. He stood there dying before my eyes that were suddenly filled with tears.

"Happy birthday, Vanessa," said Mom. "It's good to see you." We hugged. "You look—great."

"Thank you. I just had it done," I said, touching my hair.

"It's been too long."

"Yeah."

"How have you been?" asked my dad.

"Fine. And you?" What a stupid question.

"Well, not so great. That's why we're here."

"Oh ... Mr. and Mrs. Palmer, you're here." Ruth came to the rescue, hugs and kisses and welcomes for everyone. "I've got a table set up in the back where it will be quieter. Come, sit."

"Yeah, come on. Get out of the drafty doorway," I said, ushering them toward the dining room.

"Might catch pneumonia," Dad said with a laugh that was more of a cough.

"Oh, Gray," said Mom, slapping him lightly on the shoulder. She was smiling.

I had no idea why.

Thanks to Ruth and Dale, the rest of the evening went along more smoothly. We found out that there was a research group looking for nonsmoking lung cancer patients at the University of San Francisco. Dad was to go through a battery of tests and examinations to see if he qualified to try out a new form of therapy. I guess he'd run out of more traditional options. I mostly just listened and wondered what they all were thinking. Could Ruth and Dale tell what a lousy relationship we had? Was it as apparent as it felt? It was all too weird.

I was relieved that the conversation wore Dad out fairly quickly, and they had to get back to the hotel. We stood together in the doorway. More awkward hugging. Before he got into the cab, Dad handed me an envelope. "Happy Birthday, Vanessa," he said before he shut the door. "Maybe we can see each other tomorrow, after my appointments."

"Okay. Good luck." Another brilliant thing to say.

I hurried inside and put the card in my purse. I figured it was my annual Hallmark card and $50 check. I didn't open it until I was in my room that night. It was my annual Hallmark and a check. And a letter. From Dad.

Dear Vanessa,

I know that I have never written to you. You've been away from home for years, and I've never even initiated a phone call to you. I'm sorry. I guess that's what I really want to say—I'm sorry. Words are cheap. I realize that. And nothing can make up for the years that I've stayed away from you. But nevertheless, I've been thinking a lot lately. That's what you do when you've run out of all other options. You stop. You think.

I don't know what it will be like, dying. The only thing I can do now is think about what I'm going to leave behind. I think about what I wanted to do with my life and what I've actually done. I think about what I regret and wish upon wish that I could change—the one thing, if I could do it all again, that I would change. You probably think I wish Jake would not have died, and of course that is true. But I am smart enough to know that there was nothing I could have done to change that. Of all the things that I regret about my life that I was in control of, the greatest is my relationship with you. I've kept you at arm's length. I've pushed you away and pretended you weren't there. I did not understand you. You were not what I expected, so I shut you out. How can I say I'm sorry for such a thing? I don't know. All I can do is say it. I'm sorry. I'm sorry. I'm sorry.

I know that it is too little, too late, but I'm sorry, Vanessa. I was wrong. I wish I could change it. I don't have much time to make it better. But if you can find it in your heart somehow to forgive me for being a selfish fool, I'll be here, hoping to be your father for whatever time I have left. With all my love, Dad.

There was my chance. I had it in my hand, the way to be free of all the trash I'd carried around forever. I could have gone to him, fallen at his knees, and accepted his love and forgiveness and been free to get out of the self-defeating rut I had lived in for so long. But instead, I picked up my shovel and dug another six feet down.

I didn't want to be free. His apology did nothing but further ignite my rage into a fiercer burn. How dare he? How dare he come *now*, seeking a deathbed reconciliation! "I'm gonna die, so I'd better get any pesky guilt off my chest." No way. I was not going to give him the satisfaction. I wasn't about to let him off the hook, even if he was dying. It was too little, too late, and I wasn't going to give him a thing. It was *my* miserable life, and I was sticking to it, by golly. How dare he expect me to put on a smiley face and pretend it all didn't happen? No way, no sir, no how. I shoved his letter in my baggie, and sank deeper into my safe haven of self-pity.

"Vanessa. Vanessa? It's getting late and your mom's on the phone. She wants to know when you guys can get together tonight."

"I can't. I think I've got the flu," I lied.

"Oh, dear, let me get you something."

"No. I don't need anything but sleep. You'd better stay away. The last thing I want is to get you sick."

"Vanessa? How are you feeling, honey? Your parents are leaving this afternoon, and they really want to see you before they go."

"Oh, I just can't. I can't even get out of bed without feeling like I'm going to faint. Tell them I'm sorry. I'll see them next time."

"Are you sure? They'll be so disappointed. Maybe I should call a doctor."

"No, no doctor. I'll be fine in a day or two. Tell them I'm sorry."

"If you're sure."

I really should have been an actress.

I shut the door on the whole situation ... with a slam.

November 6

Dear Me,

I was a mess, plain and simple. I hated myself, I hated my parents, I hated myself for hating my parents. I loved Ruth and Dale, I loved my job, I hated myself for being so pathetic that I couldn't even enjoy the things I loved. My rope was unraveling rather quickly.

But somehow I held on. I'll never understand completely how or why. I wanted to let go. It seemed so much easier just to give up—but with my puny pinkie finger grasping the final strand of rope—God lifted me out of bed. He gave me one last chance. He had already given me lots. He's a rather patient guy. He wants everyone to know Him. But He doesn't force us. Sooner or later, you've got to choose. If I had not taken Him up on it that morning—I would have killed myself. I know that for sure.

I didn't have all my problems worked out. Actually, I didn't have *any* of them worked out. I had been in bed for a week, reliving my pathetic life and dreaming of ways to end it, when something came over me. Intuition, boredom, hunger, the need to use the bathroom? Whatever the initial urge was, the Spirit of God used it to get me up, get me dressed, and get me to church.

I went downstairs. Ruth was where she always was. She looked up from her Bible and simply said, "Dale will be here in a half hour to get you. I'm staying home today. Can I fix you some toast?"

For some reason, I didn't ask any questions. I just sat down and ate my breakfast.

"Why did He come in a manger?" the minister asked the congregation.

"Any ideas? Why was the Lord, the foreseen Savior of the world who had been prophesied about from the beginning of time, born in a barn? Placed in a manger on a bed of hay? While cows and sheep chewed their cud and did all of their other nasty business around Him? It was a barn, ladies and gentlemen. You know what a barn smells like, don't you? It was not a pretty sight."

Laughter.

"But nonetheless, that is where God chose for His Son to be born. There are no accidents with God. Why this way? Wouldn't He have avoided all kinds of problems if He had chosen some other method? Why do the Jewish people, God's chosen people, still not believe that Jesus is their Messiah? Because He didn't come as they thought

He should have. Wouldn't skeptics of Christianity have a much easier time buying it if Christ had come in mighty flames, with a flowing robe and shining sword in His hand? If He had been Superman, faster than a speeding bullet, stronger than a locomotive ... wouldn't people have an easier time believing in who He is?"

Everyone nodded in unison.

"But a baby? A tiny baby, like each of us once was—some of us more recently than others."

Laughter.

"A baby. Born in a barn, to a simple young woman and a carpenter. Why? Because He loves us so much. He humbled Himself, came to earth in the likeness of mere man, so that He could walk where we walk. So He could say, 'Been there, done that, I know what you're going through, and I love you anyway.' He saw it all, He felt it all, yet He did it all without sin, so that each one of us can have a personal relationship with Him. If He had come any other way, if everyone had believed who He was from the start, then He never would have died the death of a criminal on the cross. And if He hadn't died on the cross, then we would all be lost in our sin, destined for life separated from God, and striving in our imperfect bodies to live up to His perfection. He knows where you have been ... and He loves you anyway ... more than words from this simple man could ever express. Please stand."

We all stood. I cried. Dale and I left and went to some restaurant. We ordered soup and salad and I started:

"How do you know if God can forgive you?"

"It says so in the Bible. 'God is faithful and just to forgive all our sins,'" he said simply.

"Well, how do you know the Bible is true? There's all kinds of stuff out there that says otherwise. How do you know for sure?"

"Well, there are all kinds of historical facts about prophecies fulfilled and archeological findings that support the Bible. But I'm not a theologian, so I can't really list them for you."

"So how do you know?" I asked.

"Faith."

"Faith?"

"Yeah. Faith. I don't know what else to say."

"Okay, so He died for all the wrong stuff we've done, right?"

"Right. Putting our trust in Him doesn't make us perfect. We still blow it. But we have someone to turn to and someone to forgive us."

"How do you know He forgives you? How did you *know?*"

"Because I felt it in the depth of my soul. I know that sounds hokey, but it's true. I've heard it said this way—that all people are born with a God-shaped hole in the center of their being. We try to fill that hole with everything the world has to offer, but it never works. Some try drinking or drugs, some try sex, some try money, some try false religions, but they never are able to get rid of the empty feeling inside, until they ask the One who created them to fill it once and for all. Kind of like Cinderella's slipper. No matter how hard her stepsisters tried to squeeze their foot into it, only Cinderella's perfectly shaped foot could fill the glass slipper. And she got to be the prince's bride."

"But can't you reach the point where you've tried too many substitutes, and God finally gives up on you?"

"No. It says in the Bible that it is the will of God that everyone should come to know Him."

"Okay, I know I'm being annoying, but I keep coming back to my first question. How do you know the Bible is true?"

"How did you know the chair you are sitting in was going to hold you up?"

"What?"

"The chair you're sitting in—how did you know for sure it would hold you up?"

"I didn't, I guess."

"How'd you find out?"

"I sat in it."

"Exactly."

HMMMM.

"I heard a great illustration once," he said, breaking the silence. "Suppose a parent or a friend or someone gave you a really expensive present. They had saved and splurged on it, wanting to give you the perfect gift. They wrapped it in beautiful gold paper with a big ribbon, and gave it to you. Yet, suppose after handing it to you, you set it on your lap, admired the pretty package, and reached in your pocket to pay them for it. Would it still be a gift?"

"No."

"No, not at all. God already paid for your sins,

Vanessa. He paid for all of them, yours, mine, and everyone's before we were even born. The price was paid when Jesus Christ died on the cross. He had done nothing wrong, He was sinless, but He took our punishment by dying and then rising again to join His Father in heaven, where He waits for all of us to join Him. There is no way to pay Him back. He's given you a gift, and all He wants you to do is accept it, open it up, and let Him fill that hole you've tried to fill with so many other things."

"I don't understand it all," I said. Tears were running down my face.

"You don't have to. All you have to do is sit down. He'll take care of the rest."

"I want to sit."

"Oh, Vanessa."

I looked up at him and tears were streaming from his eyes too, but he had the most beautiful smile on his face.

"What do I do?"

"Repeat after me ... Dear Lord,"

"Dear Lord,"

"I admit to you that I am a sinner."

"I admit to you that I am a sinner."

"I know now that there is nothing I can do to take away those sins. I know that I have been trying in vain to fill the hole in my life that only You can fill. Forgive me for all I've done deliberately or unintentionally that has displeased You. I believe that Your Son, Jesus Christ, died on the cross as a payment for my sin. And I believe that He rose again and waits in heaven for me to join Him someday. I ask You to come into my heart. I surrender my will to You. I trust that You will help me to learn more about You. I thank You for what You are going to do in my life."

"Amen."

"Amen."

So there you have it. The big day. The turnaround. I wish I could say that was the happy ending of my story. That I prayed, changed, and lived happily ever after. No. Obviously not. Later I wondered what the point of being a Christian was, if I still had so much pain to go through. But now I know for certain, if I hadn't made that decision on that day, I would never have survived the pain that was waiting for me.

Part Six

November 9

Dear Me,

That was a very special Christmas. It was the first time that I realized that the holiday was more than Santa Claus and Frosty the Snowman. The incredible story of the birth of Jesus and the shepherds and wise men coming from afar bearing gifts to this tiny baby who was going to change the world became real to me. Ruth and Dale treated me like a princess, taking me to see the Christmas lights and the sights of the city. We walked arm in arm around Union Square, admiring the nativity scenes and angels that decorated many of the shop windows. We went to a sing-along *Messiah* presentation at Davies Symphony Hall. It was the first time I had been there since my disastrous audition. But it didn't bother me, as I soaked up the precious words of Handel's beautiful music.

I was falling in love. First, with this new God I had found who was real and evident in so many different ways, especially in the lives of my best friends. When I accepted Him, Ruth and Dale became even more "attractive" to me. I wanted to have the same peace and love they had in life, and for the first time I had hope that it was possible. I was also falling in love with Dale. He was everything I wanted to be and cute to boot. And though I was scared to be feeling what I was feeling for him, considering my sorry track record in relationships, somehow I knew that a relationship with him would be different.

We had already been spending all of our time together for a couple months by the time Christmas came along. It was like we suddenly realized, "Hey, we're kind of 'dating' aren't we?" On Christmas Eve, after a party at Solomon's featuring this awesome trumpet player who played Christmas carols all night, he walked me home. It was cold and clear and perfect. When we got to the steps of Ruth's house, he turned me toward him. He lifted my chin, and just like in the movies, brushed his gloved hand down my cheek. "Can I kiss you good night, Vanessa?"

Is that not the sweetest thing? It still gets me all goofy and mushy inside just thinking about it. Of course I said yes! And he did. I went inside blushing like a schoolgirl, and it took me hours to fall asleep.

Things went really fast after that. We spent all our spare time talking, learning, and growing closer to each other. I'm sure most people would think it was crazy, but it was exactly one week after that first kiss that he asked me to be his wife.

It was New Year's Eve, and Solomon's was hopping. Silver and gold streamers were all over the place. We gave out party hats and blowers to all the guests as they came in. We had champagne and sparkling cider, on the house. At the strike of midnight, blowers, noisemakers, hooting, and hollering filled the restaurant as the piano player played "Auld Lang Syne," but Dale's words were clear. "I love you, Vanessa Palmer. I have loved you since I first saw you. I made a promise to myself several years ago that I would never tell a woman I loved her until I was sure that she was the woman I wanted to marry. I wanted to be sure the words had the power they're meant to have. I'm not one to break my promises." He got down on one knee, in the middle of the toasting crowd, held my hand, and placed a perfect solitaire diamond on my finger. "Will you marry me?"

Talk about goofy! I was literally weak in the knees. I knelt down to his level, kissed his sweet mouth, and said, "Yes." It wasn't until we stood up, hugging, that we realized the whole party had stopped and they were all looking at us.

"She said yes!" he yelled. Everyone cheered. It was Hollywood!

I didn't enjoy it for too long. By the next day, I was in full panic mode. What had I done? Here was this precious, innocent, all-around-as–terrific-as-they-get guy who was somehow duped into believing that I was a good choice for a wife. He didn't even know me. I was convinced that he would find out about all of the sordid details of my past and yank the beautiful diamond right off my hand. Who could blame him? I loved him so much and I wanted it all to be perfect, but it wasn't perfect and I didn't have any idea of what to do about it.

Thank God for Ruth.

"Oh, Vanessa. Daughter! I can't tell you how thrilled I am. I can't believe it. Well, yes I can believe it, but I'm so thrilled I could hardly sleep. I could not ask for a better daughter-in-law." She was gushing. She hugged me, kissed me, spread tears all over me.

"Oh, yes you could," I said, starting to cry myself.

"What on earth do you mean by that nonsense?" she asked.

"You could do a lot better than me, that's for sure. And so could Dale."

"That's simply not true. No one is perfect—"

"Some much further from it than others," I said.

"Yes, some are. But Christ is the leveling board. In Him, we are all the same. He does not grade us from bad to worst. He just loves us and allows others to love us too. You stop that talk."

"You don't even know ... I haven't even told you everything ..."

"You sit down, dear. I have a story to tell you."

"Okay."

"Did Dale ever tell you about Maureen?"

"Yeah. They dated for awhile."

"Yes. For two years, I believe. She was a lovely girl. They met at church, and her father was a pastor of a large church in Santa Monica. She taught Sunday school and sang in the choir. There was nothing I could have ever found wrong with her as a daughter-in-law."

"And this is supposed to make me feel better?"

"Just wait. Dale was in school, he and his dad were making all kinds of plans for the future, and Dale wanted to get married. He came to us and asked what we thought of Maureen. We told him that she was lovely, wonderful, etc. But I could tell he was unsure. 'What is it, Son? You know we'll support anything you do.'

"'I know,' he said, 'it's just that I don't know. She seems perfect, but ...'

"I told him that if there were any 'buts,' he needed to wait for them to be gone. He was afraid she was going to move back to Santa Monica if he didn't ask her to marry him soon. She was going home for Spring Break the next day, and he was afraid she would decide to stay at home. I said he couldn't rush it. He left unsure."

I was listening more intently now.

"I couldn't sleep that night. I just lay in bed and worried about Dale. I thought he was going to decide in fear, not love, and I didn't want that to happen. I tossed and turned. Finally I came down to this chair, took out my Bible, and read one of my favorite verses." She opened up her Bible and handed it to me, pointing to the highlighted words of Philippians 4:6 and quoted them: 'Do not be anxious about anything, but in everything, by prayer and petition, with thanksgiving, present your requests to God.' I've always been a praying woman. But sometimes I forget how accessible God is when we pray in faith. So, I got down on my knees and prayed for Dale. I prayed that he wouldn't make any rushed decisions. I prayed that God would make it abundantly clear to him whom he was to marry. I prayed for God to seal that girl in the palm of His hands, to set her apart for Dale, to protect her from Satan's destructive plans for her life, and bring her to Dale in His perfect timing."

I glanced down at the highlighted passage.

"God told me that night that Maureen was not the one, and that He would reveal that to Dale. He told me to keep on praying for the girl who was to be Dale's wife. So I have. Every day since that spring night I've been praying for, well, for you, Vanessa."

I couldn't take my eyes off the passage. My stomach turned and my heart raced. "Is this the date you started praying?" I asked, pointing to the penciled numbers in the margin.

"Yes, dear. I always like to mark down special things like that."

The date was so familiar. I knew that date because it was the one stamped on my arrest record. I saw the face of that family that should have been dead, my car that miraculously didn't go careening over the side of Highway 1. I remembered thinking clearly that I was supposed to have died and I had been spared. Ruth's prayer saved me. I knew it for sure. That was the night I was sealed in the palm of God's hand.

Godulous.

It became clear to me that day that I was supposed to be Dale's wife. It was also clear that I had some confessing to do. I felt as though I had to spill the beans that day. And I did, at least some of them.

I asked Dale to come over to Ruth's—I needed to confess to them both. I told them about Kenneth. I told them about Alice, how she introduced me to more than just Eastern mysticism. I told them that I had made up the whole story about my fiancé because I was embarrassed to admit I had been dumped by a lesbian and that was why I wanted to kill myself. I told them how sorry and ashamed I was for deceiving them. I told Dale that I wouldn't blame him if he wanted his ring back. I told them everything. Almost.

I just couldn't tell them about the baby. I just couldn't say the words to them.

When I was finished, Dale took my hand.

"Vanessa. I forgive you. I'm glad you told me. It makes me sad that you went through so much, and I'll admit I wish you hadn't experienced those things. But when I look at you, I don't see someone with a battered and bruised past. I see in you a new creation, forgiven and set free by the grace of God, and I love you just the same." He kissed me.

I cried. Because he loved me anyway. I cried and cried and thanked him. And buried the one last unspoken morsel of truth deeper down, covered it up, and convinced myself that it didn't matter. Obviously, he loved me regardless. There was no reason to tell him now. Right?

November 10

Dear Me,

I know that most girls have a wedding planned in their heads before they are eight. I suppose they get out their Barbie and Ken dolls and plan the whole thing right down to the honeymoon in the Malibu camper. The closest thing I had to a Barbie was The Happy Family, an African-American hippie family decked out in bell bottoms and sweater vests. It had Mom, Dad, Baby, Grandma, Grandpa (who had this really cool salt and pepper beard) and a microvan. Hours of fun and a cultural education too! All this to say, I didn't have the slightest idea how to plan a wedding.

I called Mom and Dad to tell them the news. I was friendly, trying to be the good Christian daughter I was supposed to be. I just ignored the whole note incident and went on as if everything was normal and nice. Dad was really sick, and Mom didn't think she could do much to help with wedding plans or finances, which was fine. Dale and I had enough for a small service, which is what we both wanted, and Ruth was born to be a wedding planner. She thought of all the little details that would never have occurred to me. I put her in charge of everything. All I wanted was to pick out my dress. It all took six months, perfect timing for a late-June wedding.

During those six months, Dale and I went to premarital counseling every other week at the church. It was a requirement with Pastor Harvey, and I'm sure it was a fine idea. It would have been a really fine idea if I had cooperated and been totally honest with Dale during those sessions. But of course, I didn't. I just couldn't. Though I believed in forgiveness in theory, I could not believe that *everything* was forgivable. There had to be some limits, and I had surpassed them.

For our first session, we met in Pastor Harvey's office on a Monday morning. It was informal, thankfully, because I was a nervous wreck. He looked much smaller and younger then he did in the pulpit wearing his long robe. I relaxed a little. Though I had to wipe my palms on my skirt before accepting his hand to shake.

"Ah, Dale and Vanessa. You are right on time. Come on in and have a seat," he said, motioning to the tapestry-covered love seat in the corner of the room. He sat in a leather chair in front of us. We were surrounded by bookshelves that looked as if they could not possibly hold another book. I wondered how he reached the ones on the top. Perhaps they were just for looks.

"I know it's pretentious, all the books," he said, reading my gaze. "I was a psychiatrist before becoming a pastor. I got tired of the clinical side of problems and thought I'd take a stab at helping people with the spiritual side. But it took a whole new set of books to learn about that. Now it seems that I have an addiction. I don't read half of what I buy or receive as gifts, but I look smart, don't I?"

He was a regular guy. I relaxed even more.

"Let me tell you how this works. We will meet every other week for ten weeks. That will take us up to a couple of weeks before the big day. We will cover some of the basics: background, expectations of marriage, finances, conflict resolution, which ties into finances quite well, children, and of course, s-e-x. That's when it gets fun. These meetings are designed to help you address some things that you might not normally talk about in your day-to-day lives. The better you understand each other's expectations and desires for marriage, the easier it is to adjust to being officially joined, for-better-for-worse-till-death-do-you-part."

"How long will we meet?" Dale asked.

"About an hour or so. Some weeks might not take so long, others might take longer."

"How much does it cost?"

"Your tithes and offerings cover it. It's part of my job description. But I might suggest that you purchase a book or two along the way. I like books, you know, but that's it. Any other questions before we get started?"

"What if we don't pass?" Dale asked with a laugh.

"Never happened. Some were tougher than others, but everyone passes eventually, if it's meant to be, of course. No one can foresee all of the challenges of a marriage. It is hard work. But with commitment and faith in God and each other, you will both live happily ever after, despite the ups and downs. I promise. Now, let's get started. Dale, tell me about your parents' marriage."

"My parents?"

"Yep. One of the best indicators of your expectations of marriage is how you viewed your parents' union. Was it good, close, shaky, volatile?"

Dale spent the next fifteen minutes describing an Ozzie-and-Harriet household with homemade bread and Sunday school and good-night stories before being tucked in for the night. There were quarrels, over money usually, when they were young, but they lived by the verse that said not to let the sun go down on their anger, so they always made up quickly. God was the focal point of their marriage, and they taught Dale how to make Him his focal point too. He had nothing but good things to say about them.

I was not surprised by any of it. I knew it was good. I had seen the fruits of their goodness, but I was still intimidated by it when it came my turn to speak. I was embarrassed by my lack of positive things to say about what I observed of my parents' marriage. What did it say about me and my chances of a successful one?

"I suppose they love each other. I mean, they have stayed together all of these years. They lasted through some of the worst of circumstances. But they just didn't know how to show love very well, I guess." The end.

"Okay, then. You know what I love about this part of my job? Getting to know you all better and getting to see how God brings people from such different places and circumstances together as one. It's awesome the way He works, don't you think?"

We talked for a little longer about how our differences might play out in marriage and then our time was up.

"Let's pray before you go."

The following meetings were relatively painless. I was able to skim along, enjoying what I was learning about Dale and sharing a little about me along the way. Nothing too revolutionary happened. I did not feel threatened or vulnerable except for one time, when we started talking about career goals and interests.

"Are you happy with what you do, Vanessa?"

"Yes. I love the restaurant."

"Do you love the restaurant or do you love being with Dale?"

"Well, I love that, of course," I said smiling, "but I love working there too."

"So, when you were a little girl, or let's say when you were graduating from high school, you said, 'I want to be a restaurant hostess when I grow up'?"

"Well, no."

"I'm not trying to put you down, Vanessa."

He could have fooled me. I knew my face was getting red.

"Really. I'm just trying to make you think about what you do and why you do it. You have to be careful when couples work at the same business. The last thing you want to do is get ten, fifteen, twenty years down the road and realize that you're filled with all kinds of regret about how you spent your life. You don't want to have more fuel to throw on a heated argument than necessary. It's not good for anyone."

"Okay, I know what you mean. I love my job."

"Good. But just for fun, tell me what you did want to be when you were little?"

"A musician." I needed a drink of water.

"Really?"

"Yeah."

"What kind of musician? A rock star?"

"Hardly. I played the cello."

"When did you stop?" he asked.

"After my first two years of college."

"College? You were quite serious, then? Why did you quit?"

"Oh, it was silly. I finally realized that I was never going to make it so I stopped trying. It was a good hobby, but that's all."

"Do you still play?" Pastor Harvey asked.

"No. I don't even have a cello anymore. I probably wouldn't know what to do if I did," I laughed through my teeth. "It was a long time ago."

"Okay, but say she wanted to take it up again, Dale, or maybe even go back to school or something. Would you be supportive?"

"Absolutely. I wish she would. I would love to hear her play," Dale said.

"Sorry, honey. Not going to happen," I said with my best plaster smile.

I missed the cello. I hadn't realized how much until we started talking about it. The whole time there was a gnawing in the pit of my stomach. But I knew I could never return to it. It was all tied up with the rest of my garbage. I couldn't see how to separate it. All or nothing, you know.

"What about you, Dale? What did you want to be?" I asked, the master of diversion.

"Well, I did want to be an astronaut. I had this little space suit I'd run around in and I'd make a rocket ship out of boxes and stuff."

"How'd you get interested in cooking?" the pastor asked.

"I'm much better at filleting fish than physics," he said. "And I get motion sick on roller coasters. I doubt I'd do well in space."

"Well, I suppose it will be easier for her to pursue her past dreams than you, but you never know. Anything is possible," Pastor Harvey said with a smile.

"Maybe you can play in the church orchestra sometime," Dale said as we left.

"Yeah, right. That would be a sound for sore ears," I laughed.

Then came our final session.

"Well, you've made it to graduation day. We're getting pretty close to 'pronouncing you husband and wife.' How do you feel?" Pastor Harvey began our meeting.

"Great," we said.

"Today is the day you've been waiting for. The sex talk. I'm going to come right out and ask: have you two been waiting until you're official?"

"Yes."

"Great. That makes this talk so much easier. If not, I'd have to tell you guys to stop it from here on out, and believe me, once you start, it's not so easy to stop. I'm proud of you guys."

"So am I," said Dale with a smile. "It hasn't been easy to keep my hands off her." He squeezed my leg.

I hadn't had any problems.

"Now, let me tell you how this is going to go. I don't want this to be a time to describe all of your past sexual experiences. It is not a confessional. I don't want to know. But that being said, I want you two to be sure that you have laid it all out on the table with each other. The honeymoon is not the time for deep, dark secrets of any kind to surface. Especially those of the sexual variety. You don't have to tell each other all the details of every thought and deed done. But I do want to encourage you to be totally honest about where you've been and any fears you may have about where you are going. That will help you in the long run as you learn to live together sexually within the bonds of marriage."

"We've told each other everything," Dale said confidently. "She knows that I blew it a few times when I was younger, and I know that she has too. We don't have any secrets."

Just one, Dale. I'm sorry, but there is one.

"Good. I'm so glad to hear that. What about kids? Gonna have a brood?"

"Definitely. At least two," he said.

"Vanessa? Two or more?" Pastor Harvey asked.

"Yeah. That's what we want," I said. But in my gut, I didn't believe that it would ever happen. I didn't deserve a baby. But Dale did. He hadn't done anything wrong. I prayed every night that I could have one for him. He wanted a child so much.

"What about child-rearing? Are you willing to stay home with them, Vanessa? Or are you going to want to work outside the home?"

"Oh, stay home definitely."

"You okay with that, Dale? Are you willing to be the primary breadwinner?"

"Yes, sir. I'd do that now if she wanted."

"Good. Hey, maybe you could give private cello lessons on the side, Vanessa. People will pay good money for that," said Pastor Harvey with a grin.

"They'd just be wasting perfectly good money," I said. *Why wouldn't he just drop it?*

"Well, it sounds like you've got this pretty well figured out. You guys have made my job easy. I just want to finish up by telling you that God made sex. He made it for our pleasure and to procreate. But I hope you'll do it more for the pleasure. Our nursery can't handle too much more procreation! Seriously, enjoy each other. Read the Song of Solomon. It is quite a love story, you know. God is not a stick in the mud; He thought of the whole thing after all. Pretty creative if you ask me. He knows how it is best enjoyed, and He wants you two to enjoy each other immensely. Take the time to get to know each other physically, and you will enjoy a life of marital bliss."

"Oh, we will. That I can promise," Dale said. He kissed my cheek and grabbed my hand.

Such a good man.

And so on June 23, we said our "I dos" in a simple, beautiful ceremony in the church's rose garden. Dad was too sick to come. Mom had to stay with him, so it was just Ruth and a few friends from the restaurant. Everyone cried. I was so happy. I could not believe how far I'd come. I knew it had to have been God. I did not deserve such a wonderful man. He deserved so much more. But I knew he loved me, for whatever reason. And I loved him more than life.

If I'd known the problems my holding back the truth was going to cause us, I would have told him everything. If I had had any idea that my body would react to what was going on in the deepest parts of my being, I would have told him.

I had no idea—the truth really does set you free.

November 11

Dear Me,

I've never been comfortable talking about S-E-X. Mom and Dad never talked about it. The extent of

Mom's birds-and-bees talk was when I was around fifteen and she said, "Dad and I waited until we were married. You should too." No explanation, no motivation to obey, no direction.

When Kenneth and I started sleeping together, I had no religious convictions about "going all the way," although I knew I wasn't supposed to since we weren't married. Not nearly enough reason to stop the passion that overpowered every other thought or feeling. My mind had no control over the physical urges of my body when it was next to his. With Alice, I had the whole homosexual stigma in the way. I had not been raised to believe that it was socially or morally acceptable. I had never even known a lesbian, to my knowledge, prior to meeting her. Yet, the physical and emotional satisfaction I received from our relationship far outweighed any doubts I had about the "rightness" of the act itself.

Now I was almost twenty-six years old. I was married in the church to a wonderful man. God Himself was giving me the green light to fulfill the natural desires He had given us to enjoy. And I could not do it.

Everything was perfect. I had a beautiful white lace negligee from Mom, of all people. I took a long, hot bubble bath and dabbed scented oil in all the right spots. There was a fire roaring in front of the bed. Classical music was softly playing in the background. Dale was waiting expectantly on the king-sized, satin-soft bed, illuminated only by the candles that surrounded the room. He was gentle and soothing and passionate as he kissed my lips, my neck, my chest. Very seductive.

And I wanted him. My mind was wild with desire for this man. My husband. But as soon as we went past the point of preparation, my heart started to race erratically, my head pounded—screaming for it to stop, and our union was halted by excruciating pain.

"I'm sorry. I'm hurting you. Oh, Vanessa. I thought you were ready. I'm so sorry. I guess I got carried away," he gasped, trying to regain his composure.

"No, no. It's okay, you didn't do anything wrong. I guess I just need to slow down a bit." I tried desperately to calm down. *What was wrong with me?*

We slowed down. He was so gentle. He tried so hard, but I couldn't let it happen. My body refused to cooperate. He rolled over in frustration.

"I'm sorry," I said softly.

"Shhh. Don't be sorry. I guess it's going to take a little time to get things right."

"Yeah," I said not able to stop the tears from spilling out of the corners of my eyes. I couldn't believe this was happening.

"Are you okay?" he asked shyly.

"Yeah. I guess. I don't know what's wrong with me. It just hurts so bad. It's like I don't work or something."

"Oh, you work all right." He tried to sound funny. "Maybe you're just tired. It's been a long day. Why don't we get some rest? We can try again in the morning." He kissed my hair.

"Okay."

"We've got a lifetime to figure this out. And just think how much fun it will be practicing."

It wasn't any better in the morning.

Or that night.

Or the next morning.

We returned to his apartment Monday morning, frustrated but trying to hide it. Scared, but not willing to address the problem. I think we were both happy to go back to work that afternoon.

He hugged me before we left for work. "It's going to be okay, Vanessa. We are going to get through this. 'For better and for worse,' remember? I've waited this long. What's a few more days?"

After three weeks, he suggested that I see a doctor.

"Dyspareunia," (or some horrible D disease—diarrhea, diphtheria ... they all sound so unpleasant) said the doctor after reading my complaint in my chart. "It is rather common and caused by different things, usually easy to treat. Sex isn't supposed to hurt, so we'll try to keep it from doing so, okay?"

"Okay," I said. Nervous as heck. At least she was a woman. That helped a little.

"Now, lay back and let's take a look. Relax, relax ... breathe, I know it's uncomfortable, but I'll be done shortly."

Not soon enough.

"I'm going to take a culture to be sure infection of some sort isn't the problem. Everything looks okay, but it's always good to check."

I didn't care what she did at that point.

"Good, we're almost finished. I'm just going to feel

around a bit. Okay, now breathe, breathe. We're done. You did great."

Yeah, right.

"Go ahead and sit up."

Gladly.

"Well, Vanessa. Everything seems in order."

"I guess that's a relief."

"There's a little scarring on your cervix, but I don't think that is causing you any trouble. Your uterus is right where it's supposed to be, and I don't see any signs of infection."

"So, what does that mean?" I asked.

"Well, I don't know. Sometimes women get so nervous about sex that they involuntarily close off the muscles down there, making it impossible. Do you feel anxious about sex?"

"A little, I guess," I lied. I assumed if she knew I felt like I was going to have a heart attack every time, she would want to run more tests.

"That's normal. Let's call your husband in, and I'll tell you what we're going to try. He's going to have to participate as well. Okay?"

"Okay."

"Go ahead and get dressed. I'll be back with him in a minute."

I did what I was told, hopeful that maybe she was going to have a magic potion to make this nightmare go away.

Dale knocked and came in tentatively, followed by the doctor.

"You okay?" First he asked me, then turned toward the doctor.

"Yes, she seems fine."

I couldn't tell if he thought that was good or bad news. I know he wanted an answer.

"I think she is having a problem with what we doctors term 'vaginismus.'"

"That doesn't sound good." He seemed embarrassed.

"No, it simply is a term to describe muscle spasms that prevent sexual penetration. It's kind of like a charley horse, only further up."

"What causes it?"

"Lots of things, but usually anxiety."

He looked at me.

I shrugged.

"Vanessa has admitted to me that she might feel a little apprehensive about sex. I'm going to let you both talk about that however you want. But in the meantime, I'm going to send you home with this information about different relaxation techniques and exercises you can both do to try and loosen things up a bit."

Now he really looked embarrassed.

"It might take some time, but it can also be fun. I want to see you back in a month to see how it's going, okay?"

"Okay." In unison.

"Thank you, doctor," Dale said. He took our packet of "magic potion," and we drove home. He was ready to make it happen.

I tried.

We relaxed. We massaged and caressed. We did

everything we were supposed to do. Every time it got a little closer, I stopped it. Every time I stopped it, I felt worse about myself and more sorry for Dale. I'd get more and more nervous, anticipating failure, making the situation even worse.

Dale was patient. I was pathetic. Next he suggested prayer.

"Prayer? We've been praying," I said one morning in frustration.

"We need to ask for someone else to pray for us. 'Whereever two or more are gathered in my name, I will do it,' you know?"

"I know, Dale. But I'm too embarrassed. Who are you going to ask? Pastor Harvey?"

"I was thinking that."

"No. I can't, Dale. Please."

"Okay. Then Mom."

"Oh, Dale—"

"Come on, Vanessa. She knows something is wrong anyway. I don't think either of us are hiding it very well at this point."

He was right. Dale looked tired and tense. He walked with his jaw clenched and he smiled a lot less than usual. He had even yelled at one of the waitresses for messing up an order. He was not himself. I had dark circles under my eyes that I could not hide. I was losing weight. I was tired. "Okay," I finally said. "Ask your Mom to pray. She's probably already doing it."

"Yeah, probably. I love you, Vanessa," he said.

"I don't know why."

"Because we were made for each other, remember?"

Things just had to get better.

They got worse.

I would talk myself into doing better throughout the day. Telling myself how much I loved him, how much he loved me, that sex was a good thing, nothing was wrong with it, he needed it, I needed it ... what was my problem? I'd imagine what it would be like, to finally give in and truly become Dale's wife. It felt so good in my mind.

Dale did everything right. He'd come up behind me at work and whisper how beautiful I was in my ear. He'd catch me in the kitchen and nuzzle my neck, caress my back, do all the things he was supposed to do to make me ready and willing when bedtime finally rolled around. I would be ready and willing. And then I'd stop. Dale would turn over. We'd sleep alone in the same bed.

Every night, I'd stay awake listening to the darkness in my heart. It told me I was worthless, that I was ruining a good man, that I was completely selfish to make him stay with me, that I always had been selfish, always would be. I told myself that I was getting punished for killing my baby. I was only getting what I deserved. And night after night I believed it more and more. All I had learned about God's love and forgiveness seeped out of me little by little. I was falling backward, losing ground, and I had no idea where I'd land.

After three months—three very long months—Dale finally lost it. He had filled our bedroom with tiny candles everywhere. He made my favorite dinner and played my favorite music. We were getting to that point, the moment where everything normally fell apart, and it seemed like it was finally going to work ... and of course it didn't.

"God help me, Vanessa! I just don't know what to do anymore!" Dale yelled as he pulled on his boxers and stormed around the room blowing out all of the candles.

He had never yelled at me before. I was scared.

"It's me. Isn't it? You just aren't attracted to me."

"No," I cried.

"Yes it is. It must be. You are comparing me to what's-his-name. Is that it?"

"Dale ..."

"Please don't tell me it's her? Do you want to be with her again? Is that it?"

"No, Dale. No. Stop. It's not you. It's me. It's me. It's always been me!" I was panicking now, pounding my hands on my head, trying to clear my thoughts.

"I can't take it, Vanessa. I just don't know what to do anymore." He was crying—grieving and frustrated. He put on his clothes, tied his shoes, and left.

The apartment was so quiet. And dark. I lay quietly in bed and listened for the street noises through our open window. But I could not hear anything. Nothing but the steady roll of darkness, like storm clouds, as it overshadowed any light that was left in me. The darkness took control from the center of my being. It told me that I could not change. It told me that God was finished with me. It told me that I had been trying to fool everyone all this time, but that the gig was up. It told me that I should have finished the job before I met Dale. It told me to go to the store at the corner and buy a fifth of vodka. It told me that I was through. And I listened to every word it said. The darkness had won.

I came back to the apartment with my bottle. The room still smelled of candle wax. I took out my bag of pills. I found a pad of paper. A pen. I wrote:

Dearest Dale,

I'm sorry.

I suppose that is a silly thing to say, but I don't know what else to tell you. You deserve an explanation. I will try to give you one. I have not been honest with you. With myself. With anyone. But there's no time for secrets now.

The last time I let someone love me, he left. That hurt, but I do not regret him leaving me. What I do regret, what I would do anything in this world to change, is that when I was with him, we made a baby. And because I didn't want to lose him, I killed it. I killed my baby.

Who does a thing like that? You deserve a better love, a purer love—a love I cannot give. I know I should have told you. I should never have let it go so far. But I thought I could change it. I thought if I did all the right things, I could make it right. I was wrong. I'm so sorry for ever coming into your life. I don't expect you to forgive me. I don't want you to. But nevertheless, I'm sorry. I love you, Dale. Thank you for loving me. Thank you for showing me God. I'm just so sorry it was too late for me.

And then I did it. I actually did what I had thought about for years. I took the pills. I swallowed them with the whole bottle of vodka. And I fell asleep, fully expecting to wake up in whatever eternity there was for baby killers.

Thank God for the weakening effect time has on prescription drugs and for the goodness in my husband's heart that brought him back to the apartment just moments after I passed out on our bed.

November 12

Dear Me,

Dale drove me to the hospital. They pumped my stomach, kept me on oxygen, and got all of my vital statistics up to snuff. I vaguely remember floating in and out of consciousness, the sound of beeps and pumps, and Dale crying. Part of me wanted to wake all the way up, the rest wanted to sleep. My head hurt and my stomach hurt. But nothing compared to the grief I felt hearing Dale cry. I couldn't understand why he was there. *Hadn't he found my note?*

After three days, I had to wake up. I had no control over it. And Dale was still there, by my side, kissing my hand.

"Hi there, honey. I'm here."

"Hi," I said. My throat was raw.

"Don't talk. Just rest. But don't sleep. Stay with me a little while. I've missed you."

"But—"

"Shh. Don't talk. I love you, Vanessa."

"But—"

He kissed me. He knelt down and put his mouth to my ear. "I forgive you, Vanessa. I forgive you," he said in tears.

I just closed my eyes and wept. Hot tears pooled in my ears and spilled out onto the stiff white pillowcase.

After I had stayed awake for a suitable period of time, they moved me.

To the psychiatric ward.

I was placed in a practically empty room, starkly white and devoid of anything that might be used to take a life—specifically my own. I could not leave the room without permission. I could not receive any guests. Two nurses ushered me to an office, which was nearly as sterile as my room, where a small, mustached, squinty-eyed man asked me all kinds of questions about my childhood, my adulthood, my fears, my thoughts, and why I had swallowed a bag of pills with vodka. I didn't want to talk to him, but I didn't want to stay in that part of the hospital either, so I cooperated just barely enough to satisfy him.

People were always screaming in there. Men would bang their heads against the walls and women would moan and pull at their hair. It was a lonely, humiliating reality. I was glad I could stay in my white room most of the time. I guess I progressed pretty well, or perhaps I was simply much better off than most of the occupants.

Three days after I was admitted, Dale and Ruth came

and told me they had found a better place for me. A small hospital in San Rafael had a Christian psychiatric unit and they had a bed available. They moved me that day. I was in a numb daze. I couldn't really process all that was happening. All I knew was that I had not succeeded in killing myself; therefore God must have wanted me alive for something. I did love Dale, and he was still there with me, despite my confession. I didn't understand it, but I was willing to do whatever they asked me to do in order to figure it all out.

My next hospital experience was much more pleasant than the first. I guess that's good—I was there for two months.

November 14

Dear Me,

I said the next experience was more pleasant than the first. That is true. But this was entirely a matter of perspective. I'm sure no one would call any stay in a psychiatric hospital "pleasant." But with everything considered, the Olive Branch unit of St. Michael's Hospital was tolerable, especially for someone as confused as I was.

Olive Branch. It was named for the story of Noah and the Ark. Noah sent three doves out to see if the floodwaters had receded from the land. The first dove came back with nothing. The second dove came back with an olive branch in his beak, a sign that land was visible somewhere. The third dove never returned—having found a better place to live. Such was the philosophy of the Olive Branch. We had all been the first dove, looking every which way for signs of hope, but coming up empty-handed again and again. We were there to find hope, healing, and the skills needed to be sent out into the world once more, never to return, because we had found better places and better ways to live.

In some aspects, the "Branch" was like any other psych ward. We couldn't have anything—belts, razors, nail clippers. We were always protected from ourselves and our darkness. We couldn't go anywhere, even the bathroom, without permission and, in some cases, an escort. We had activity time. I made a nice ceramic pot and a Christmas ornament shaped like a reindeer. Can't wait to tell my kids where they came from!

But the biggest difference about the Branch was the type of counseling we received. We weren't just medicated, though there was plenty of Prozac and Xanax distributed. But we weren't simply allowed to spout our woes and lament about how bad the world had treated us and how we'd been dealt a lousy hand in the game of life. Instead, the staff believed there was a three-pronged wheel involved in mental illness: physical, emotional, and spiritual. We were given medication to try to control the physical imbalances or faulty synapses that might be affecting us. With that under control, we were able to better deal with the emotional and spiritual aspects of our "illness." We went to daily individual counseling sessions. This was lay-down-on-the-couch-and-tell-me-about-your-childhood type of stuff. Then we would meet in large-group and small-group sessions for more "intervention" and Bible study.

This is where I met Doug.

We began by talking about how I had gotten to the point of suicide. How and what I had suppressed, what I was thinking, how long I had been thinking that way, etc. It's kind of hard to remember exactly what went on in those early sessions. But I do remember that I no longer held back. I knew I had nothing—or perhaps I had everything—to lose.

Day by day, I opened the floodgates to the hidden reservoirs of my mind.

Bible study, without trying to trivialize it, basically worked to rewire our thought processes to be healthy and based on the Truth of God's Word, not the faulty, self-degrading lies we had come to believe and live by. It was intense—challenging us that, if we truly believed in God and what He did to save us from our miserable selves, then we needed to live like it. We learned what God wanted in His relationship with us, that He in fact *wanted* a relationship with us, and how we could be healed by that relationship.

I expected my problems to get resolved quickly. After all, my biggest mistake was hiding my mistakes.... I figured that once I let the cat out of the bag, healing would be close behind. Right?

Wrong!

I already believed all the stuff about God's love. I knew He loved me—why else would He have given me so many chances to get it right? I knew He had brought Dale into my life and that He had given Dale the strength to stick by me through the mess I'd made.

So? What was my problem?

I got a bit frustrated with the process of figuring it out.

"I don't feel like I'm making much progress," I said to Doug after my first month of regular sessions.

"Why not?"

"It just seems like I'm stuck now. I don't know where to go from here."

"What are you feeling?" he asked in the way counselors love to ask.

"I don't know."

"'I don't know' has no wings; it won't fly in here."

"I know, I know, you've said that before."

"It's hard to come up with new ones."

"Okay. I'm scared."

"Of what?"

"Of revealing whatever it is that's holding me back, I guess."

"You know that there can be no darkness in God's perfect light. He won't let anything 'dark' remain hidden."

"I know. That's what I'm scared of."

"What?"

"The light."

"Ah. Good. Think about what it feels like when you come into a bright room from the dark. At first you can't see anything but a bunch of blotches and outlines, your eyes hurt, you squint. But after a while, you adjust. It becomes clear. And it's a whole lot easier to get around."

"Okay. I'm willing. Whatever it takes. I don't want to hide anymore."

"Well, that's half the battle won. You'll get through it, Vanessa. I promise."

"Okay. I'm ready."

Over the following weeks, Doug slowly broke through the layers.

Starting from the beginning—my childhood, my ambition, Jake's life, Jake's death, UOP ...

"So, you think that your parents only let you go away to school to get rid of you?"

"Yes."

"They figured if they couldn't have Jake, they might as well have no children?"

"Something like that."

"You don't think they sent you there to fulfill your dreams."

"No."

"Perhaps they saw their son's future, his dreams vanish in an instant, and they realized they shouldn't hold you back. Maybe they wanted to see you succeed because Jake never would. Is that possible?"

"I don't know. I doubt it."

"Did you ever talk to them about it?"

"No."

"Why not?"

"I don't know. We never talked about anything."

"Why?"

"I don't know. We just didn't," I started to yell.

"Okay. Okay. I'm not trying to make you mad. I just want you to consider that things aren't always how we believe them to be. Sometimes we get so hurt that we don't see straight. And then we let the bitterness take root in our hearts, and we become chronically blind. All I want you to consider is—if you didn't talk about it, how could you know what they were thinking? Keep your mind open to other possibilities. Okay? Can you do that for me?"

"I guess so. I'll try." I slumped in my chair.

"That's all I ask. Go on."

On and on we went, reliving and retelling things I had not allowed myself to think of for years. Finding my "line" in school, feeling the first thrills of success as a musician, Kenneth. Even the mention of his name made my throat constrict and my skin get hot. Of course, this did not go unnoticed.

"Why does it make you so mad to talk about him?"

"I'm not mad."

"You're not?"

"I don't know. It's just, he took it all away from me."

"What?"

"Everything."

"Okay. You're going to make me work for it. I can do that. I get the feeling that you consider Kenneth to be the main reason you were succeeding in your musical career. Is that true?"

"Yeah, he set up my auditions and performances, he chose my music, he did pretty much everything."

"Did he stand behind stage and play the cello while you moved your fingers and bow in front of the audience?"

"No," I laughed.

"Did he practice for you, sing the tunes in your head as you walked and ate and slept? Did he make you good?"

"No. Of course not."

"Would you have succeeded without him?"

"I don't know."

"Did you have what it took, musically, to play the cello professionally?"

"Yes."

"Did Kenneth make you good?"

"No."

"Did Kenneth make you quit?"

"Yes."

"How?"

"Because after what happened, I couldn't play anymore."

"After what happened?"

"You know."

"Maybe. But now it's your turn to work. After what happened?"

"He made me get an abortion."

"He did? How did he make you do it?"

I forced myself to keep talking. "He scheduled it. I thought we would be able to keep the baby. We were supposed to stay together forever, happily ever after, you know. He never even considered it. He called, he scheduled, he drove me, he picked me up."

"Did you ever tell him that you didn't want to do it?"

I didn't answer.

"Did you tell him that you didn't want to do it, that you thought it was wrong, that you couldn't go through with it?"

Silence.

"And after all your protesting, he tied up your arms, taped your screaming mouth shut, and took you under force to the abortion clinic to get rid of the problem? Is that what happened?"

"NO! NO! NO!" I screamed. "He didn't do that. He didn't make me. I was too scared and too stupid to say anything, so I went. I went and stuck my legs in stirrups and let someone suck the life out of me. Okay. It was me. I did it." I fell to the floor in tears.

November 17

Dear Me,

Each session revealed a little more of the pattern I had developed throughout my life. Like an onion, with one layer after another being peeled away—and with a lot of tears—I started to open up, into the depth of my soul. Through Doug's words, Dale's love, and God's grace, the Light began to break through.

I started to understand that we are all given a set of circumstances, some good and some bad. But we also are given the choice to deal with those circumstances either positively or negatively. I didn't choose the right way. I had considered myself the victim, the poor misunderstood soul no one loved. My parents weren't perfect. They had made a lot of mistakes. But they had done their best, and I had never allowed myself to see any of the good parts. Instead of trying to help them understand me, I harbored anger and resentment against them, sabotaging our relationship. Instead of proving myself through hard work and determination, I cowered in the shadow of Jake, and then Kenneth, to make myself feel better. When things got bad and I was left unprotected, I would run and try to find a new shelter.

It wasn't until I found Jesus that my methods began to fail me. When I gave my heart to Him, He demanded that I give up all other shelters. He demanded that I throw off all my old ways, including resentment, anger, self-loathing, and so on. When I did not give it up, I put a wall between us, which affected my marriage, stole intimacy, and nearly took my life. I was given yet another chance, and I was determined not to blow it again.

For weeks, we met with Doug. He taught me how to grieve properly for my baby. We even had a memorial service in the hospital's chapel to finally put him to rest. After I'd made enough progress to be released from the hospital, I went once, sometimes twice a week to his office. Hour after hour spent uncovering old ways of thinking and working to replace them with new ways. I felt good. I knew we were getting somewhere, but I was still holding something back. I could not consummate my marriage to Dale, and I knew he was growing weary. But he pressed on with me, through two more long months, as we peeled down to the heart of the matter.

"I'm not going to get into a political debate or even a moral discourse on the issue of abortion, Vanessa. You probably think you are the only one I have seen who has struggled like this with a past abortion."

I shrugged. *Perhaps.*

"Well, you're not. I wish I could tell you it is rare, but I have counseled scores of women who have experienced one form or another of what mental health professionals now are calling Post-Abortion Syndrome."

"Really?"

"Yes, really. It is a form of Post-Traumatic Stress Disorder, and it manifests in many different ways, including drug or alcohol abuse, sleep disturbances, suicidal thoughts, and disrupted intimacy. Sound familiar?"

"Yeah."

"I'm not going to argue about a woman's right to choose, when is a life a life, what about rape and incest, or what about the mother's life. Morality versus politics. The fact that so many women have such significant psychological damage and long-lasting emotional scars after an abortion, regardless of the circumstances behind it, is enough proof for me that it is wrong. What a woman often believes to be the quickest way to take care of a problem sadly ends up to be the cause of many greater, seemingly unrelated problems in the future. You, I know, can attest to that fact."

More tears. I'm always surprised that I don't run out of them.

"If you could change it, you would, right?"

"Definitely."

"If you could roll back the proverbial hands of time and step back on the UOP campus during the end of your freshman year, knowing what you know now, you would do it differently, wouldn't you?"

"Yes." I had my eyes closed, trying to imagine what it would be like.

"Can you do that?"

"No."

"Can you change what happened since then?"

"No."

"Can you make anything good come out of it?"

"No."

"God can."

I opened my eyes.

"He already has."

"What do you mean?"

"Do you see the man sitting next to you?" He nodded at Dale.

I grabbed his hand. "Yes."

"Do you see that ring on your finger? The home where you live, the Bible that you read. Are these good things?"

"The best. I thank God for them all the time."

"Would they be here if things had happened differently?"

"I don't know."

"If you had married Kenneth, had a baby at nineteen, gone off to New York or Paris or wherever—would you be here?"

"No."

"Do you believe that Dale is God's choice for your husband?"

"Absolutely."

"Well, then. God can make treasure out of trash. He's done it before, and He continues to do it every day as His people go on making wrong choices and coming back to Him for forgiveness."

I'd never thought of it that way.

"I'm not saying that it was God's perfect will for you to have an abortion or any of the other mistakes you've made in your life—it's not. But I am saying that He is bigger than all of it. He can pick up the broken pieces of the messes we make. All He wants is for us to ask Him for forgiveness. And his forgiveness is once and for all. 'As far as the east is from the west, so far as He removed our transgressions from us.' Remember?"

"How?" I cried.

"How what?"

"How do you let Him forgive you? How do you believe He will?"

"How do you not?"

I stared at him.

"Do you believe that God loves you?"

"Yes."

"Do you believe that He sent His only Son, Jesus, to walk perfectly on this earth as a man, without sin, only to die a horrible, painful death to pay the penalty for our sins?"

"Yes."

"Do you?"

"Yes, of course."

"But I suppose what He did just wasn't quite good enough for *you*?"

"What?"

"You heard me. His death just wasn't enough for Vanessa. In fact it should say in the Bible, 'I came that you all may have life—that is all but Vanessa. What she did was just too bad ...'"

"No, I just—"

"You just what? You want more? He needs to be killed over and over again in order to be a sufficient sacrifice for your sins? Once wasn't enough?"

I couldn't speak. I couldn't defend myself. He was absolutely right. All of the time I spent denying God's forgiveness of my sins, holding onto the really bad ones, saying that I was just too awful to deserve to be forgiven—what I was really saying was that I was too good for it. Maybe His death on the cross was enough for the rest of the world, but not for me.

At that moment, I literally wailed to God to forgive me. I fell flat on my face and wailed. Once and for all pleading with Him to take away my sins. I promised not to take them back. He had suffered enough for me.

The light broke through and the darkness was gone. It sounds melodramatic, but it was true. I was finally free. The weight was gone—nailed for good to the cross of Calvary.

Dale and I drove home. I was exhausted. Every muscle in my body ached, worn down and beaten, but my soul was free. And for the first time I was free to love and be loved completely without fear.

That night, I became Dale's wife.

Sleep (and not sleeping) that night was sweet. Warm and secure. I was a bit surprised when the dream started—

It was just like always. I sat on the porch, rocking my precious baby in my arms, when I heard my name being called from the distance. I sat my baby down and walked toward the voice, the figure in the distance. When the baby started to cry, I was torn between going forward or turning back, but I kept following the voice.

Then it changed.

When I got to the figure, I looked at his face. First it was Kenneth. Then it changed to my father. Lastly, I looked into the eyes of Jesus. He grabbed my hands, turned me around, and we walked back to the porch. Just as the crying baby was about to fall, to break into the horrid pieces that had haunted my mind for years, Jesus bent down and picked him up. He held the baby to His chest and walked away. Ascending as He walked into the clouds. Holding my child in His arms.

I truly believe that the Spirit of God met me in my dream that night, finalizing my release. I knew my child was with Jesus. I never had the dream again.

I woke up and knew what I had to do next. My work still wasn't finished.

"Dale. Dale, honey, wake up." I shook my husband awake.

"What. What's wrong?" He turned over and looked at the clock. 4:00 AM.

"Nothing's wrong. But you need to get up."

"It's the middle of the night."

"I know, I'm sorry. But we've got to go."

"Where?"

"Home."

November 18

Dear Me,

I made Dale cross over to Highway 1 when we got to Willits.

"I thought you wanted to get there in a hurry," he said.

"I do. But there's somewhere I want to stop first."

"Whatever you say. You dragged me out of bed in the

middle of the night. I guess I shouldn't start asking questions now," he smiled.

"Thank you."

"I love you, Vanessa."

"I love you too."

We stopped at Glass Beach.

It's a little inlet on the Northern California Coast in Fort Bragg. My parents took me there when I was young. I didn't think it was anything particularly special then.

But it's not your ordinary beach. The ground is not covered with sand or pebbles, but an assortment of colorful, rounded, smooth pieces of glass. Glass Beach was once a dump. The old newspapers, rotten bananas, and soda cans were swept away. But the pieces of broken glass remained under the mighty force of the Pacific Ocean, and were changed into something unique and beautiful. Like nothing you've ever seen before.

Like me.

It was clear that my life had become a waste dump, broken and discarded. I had spent years hiding, sharp and jagged, trying to avoid the pounding waves. I wanted to unearth that golden piece of treasure that would acquit me of all wrongdoing.

I never found it. Instead, I finally came to realize that I could blame no one but myself. I had made my choices—my proverbial bed to lie in—and had blown it. Not the glorious absolution I was looking for. But somehow better. For I knew now that I did not need to change all that had happened in my life. No. Instead I was going to stand in front of the waves and allow them to buffer me into the unique treasure I was born to be. Treasure out of trash.

I took an empty soda bottle from the car, washed it out in the ocean, and filled it with the colorful pieces of glass. Then we drove home … to Arcata.

We arrived just in time. Mom met us at the door, shocked to see us.

"I can't believe you're actually here. He's been asking for you over and over. How did you know?"

"I didn't. Why didn't you call?"

"Would you have come?"

I couldn't say anything.

"But you're here now, and with your dear husband. Your dad will be so happy. Come. Come in."

She took us by the hand, and I could feel every bone in her cold fingers.

"We moved him down here when the trip up and down the stairs got too much for him."

In the center of the living room, turned toward the window and the sea was a hospital bed. Attached to the bed were oxygen machines and IVs, monitors and tubes. And in the middle of it all was my father, who looked no bigger than a child.

"Daddy." I cried and ran to his side.

He looked at me, first confused, and then amazed. His blue eyes filled like my own. "You're here? Vanessa came, Helen. She came."

"I know, dear. She came."

"Thank you," he said. The simple sentence sent him into a ten-minute fit of coughing that I thought was going to kill him.

"I'm sorry," I said as he tried to stop.

"No. It's normal," said Mom. "He just doesn't have much lung left. He's okay."

"No. I'm sorry," I said to him.

He looked up at me.

I knelt at his side. I held his hand. He was so small.

"I'm so sorry, Vanessa." His voice was barely a whisper.

"Shh, Dad. You don't have to say it again. I know. I've known. Now I accept it."

Tears fell.

"Now it is my turn. I'm sorry, Dad. It's so little, but it's all I can say. I'm sorry and—I love you."

He put his hand on my head and patted it slowly. "No time for tears, Nessa. No time for tears."

He fell asleep. I sat next to him all day and slept on the couch next to his bed all night. I didn't want to leave his side.

Early the next morning, his coughing woke me up. Mom was already at his side, giving him medicine and changing his sheets. Dale was in the kitchen fixing coffee.

"Where's Nessa?"

"I'm right here, Dad. I'm here." I stood close to his bed.

"Will you do something for me?"

"Of course, Dad. What is it?"

"Play for me."

"What?"

"Play your cello for me."

I was stunned. "I can't, Dad. I haven't played for years. I don't even have a—"

"Yes. It's over there." His head motioned slightly toward the opposite wall. Next to the piano was my old cello. The cello Dad had bought me in junior high, which I had stored in the attic after Kenneth gave me the new one.

I looked at my mom.

"He asked me to bring it down a few weeks ago."

"But—"

"Please, Nessa. Play for me."

I walked to the piano and picked up the instrument. I ran my palm down the brown wood and plucked the strings. Instinctively, I twisted the pegs, amazed that my ear could still hear the right pitch.

Dale moved a chair in behind me.

I picked up the bow.

I looked up toward heaven and thanked my God for bringing me there for this moment, down that long, long road.

I sat down.

And I played ...

Readers' Guide

For Personal Reflection
or Group Discussion

Readers' Guide

1. Have you ever kept a journal? What was its purpose? Did it help?

2. No matter how hard we try not to be like our mothers or fathers, each of us is influenced, positively or negatively, by the people who raise us. How do you think your upbringing has impacted who you are today?

3. How much of what happens to you do you think is a direct result of your choices and actions as opposed to mere fate?

4. Look at Jeremiah 29:11, Galatians 1:14, Ephesians 1:4 and Deuteronomy 30:19–20, Joshua 24:15. How do you reconcile these two seemingly opposite points of view? Look at Jeremiah 29:12–13 for help.

5. What do you consider to be one of your own life-defining moments or experiences? Is there a specific event that you believe has greatly influenced who you are today?

6. What do you think is the purpose of grief? Look at these verses that speak to this process: John 16:20 and Lamentations 3:22–32.

7. Vanessa had a lot of trouble trusting her decision-making ability. How do you make decisions? Do you flip a coin? Trust in trial and error? Use eeny-meeny-miney-moe?

8. Do you believe God can help you make right decisions? Read Psalm 32:8, Proverbs 3:5–6, and Isaiah 32:19–21.

9. Have you had a negative experience with a Christian or church? Do you hold Christians to higher standards of behavior? Why or why not?

10. What characteristics do you believe should be evident in someone who professes to be a Christian? (Use these verses to help lead the discussion: Rom. 12:1–2, Eph. 5:15–17, Phil. 1:27, Titus 2:7, and 1 John 2:6).

11. What should have been Vanessa's first clue of problems with Kenneth?

12. How important is the act of listening in relationships?

13. What are the benefits of holding our tongues and opening our ears? (see Prov. 18:2, 13; James 3:2).

14. What nonreligious objections to abortion seem valid to you?

15. Is everything that is legal also right? Explain your answer.

16. Discuss how these verses speak to the issue of abortion: Psalm 139:13–14, Isaiah 46:3, Jeremiah 1:4–5, and Mark 10:14, 16.

17. What hope does God offer for those who have already had an abortion? Consider Isaiah 43:25, 44:22, and 1 John 1:9.

18. Vanessa was quite good at altering her reality. Is it okay to tell little white lies if they don't hurt anyone else? Why or why not?

19. What do these verses say about lying: Proverbs 6:16–19, Proverbs 12:19, Jeremiah 9:5–6, and Romans 3:13?

20. List methods people use to cover up their pain.

21. Have you ever had a habit or compulsion that, despite your best efforts, you couldn't break on your own?

22. Do you think it is ever possible to truly be free from such addictions?

23. Read Numbers 22:21–29. Why do you think God opened the donkey's mouth?

24. Read Exodus 3:1–4, 10. Why the burning bush?

25. Read 2 Kings 4:1–7. If Elisha had handed her a bag of gold coins, would she have learned the amazing power of God to provide for all of her needs? Why do you think He chose the bottles of oil to show her His provision?

26. Do you think miracles still happen today? Why or why not?

27. Do you have good memories of a bad time in your life? Do wrong choices look wrong when making them? (Read Gen. 3:6; Prov. 9:17, 14:12.)

28. What, in your opinion, does it mean to be "spiritual"?

29. Can all religions be right?

30. What does the Bible say in John 14:6 and John 1:14?

31. In your own spiritual journey, have you been more influenced by things you've read in books or others' actions and behaviors you've witnessed? Why do you think that's true?

32. How do you react when someone goes out of his way to be nice to you?

33. What do you think is the difference between joy and happiness?

34. Can you hide from your past, or does it always come back to bite you? Look at Ecclesiastes 12:14, Isaiah 29:15–16, and Luke 12:2–3.

35. What keeps us from forgiving?

36. Discuss the negative effects not forgiving others have had on your own life.

37. Can you relate to Glass Beach? Can God make treasure out of trash? Read 2 Corinthians 3:18, Ephesians 4:24, and Philippians 3:21.

38. Why do you think Vanessa could finally forgive her father?

39. What else did Vanessa's understanding of God's love for her allow her to do?

40. What might an understanding of God's love allow you to do?

I chose the name Vanessa for this story because it means butterfly. It is my belief that God is willing and waiting to turn each of us into a beautiful new creation if we are willing to submit to the transforming power of His cocoon. Keep on seeking, keep on asking Him to show you the Truth, keep on knocking at His door. He's waiting for you.

The Word at Work Around the World

A vital part of Cook Communications Ministries is our international outreach, Cook Communications Ministries International (CCMI). Your purchase of this book, and of other books and Christian-growth products from Cook, enables CCMI to provide Bibles and Christian literature to people in more than 150 languages in 65 countries.

Cook Communications Ministries is a not-for-profit, self-supporting organization. Revenues from sales of our books, Bible curricula, and other church and home products not only fund our U.S. ministry, but also fund our CCMI ministry around the world. One hundred percent of donations to CCMI go to our international literature programs.

CCMI reaches out internationally in three ways:

- Our premier International Christian Publishing Institute (ICPI) trains leaders from nationally led publishing houses around the world.

- We provide literature for pastors, evangelists, and Christian workers in their national language.

- We reach people at risk—refugees, AIDS victims, street children, and famine victims—with God's Word.

Word Power, God's Power

Faith Kidz, RiverOak, Honor, Life Journey, Victor, NexGen — every time you purchase a book produced by Cook Communications Ministries, you not only meet a vital personal need in your life or in the life of someone you love, but you're also a part of ministering to José in Colombia, Humberto in Chile, Gousa in India, or Lidiane in Brazil. You help make it possible for a pastor in China, a child in Peru, or a mother in West Africa to enjoy a life-changing book. And because you helped, children and adults around the world are learning God's Word and walking in his ways.

Thank you for your partnership in helping to disciple the world. May God bless you with the power of his Word in your life.

For more information about our international ministries, visit www.ccmi.org.

Additional copies of *Dear Me*
and other RiverOak titles are available
from your local bookseller.

If you have enjoyed this book,
or if it has had an impact on your life,
we would like to hear from you.

Please contact us at:

RiverOak Books
Cook Communications Ministries, Dept. 201
4050 Lee Vance View
Colorado Springs, CO 80918

Or visit our Web site:
www.cookministries.com